I0720389

The Derbyshire Set – Book 3

Regency Historical Romance

The Viscount's Unsuitable Affair

Arietta Richmond

Dreamstone Publishing © 2015

www.dreamstonepublishing.com

ISBN-13: 978-1-925499-54-4

Books by Arietta Richmond

His Majesty's Hounds

Claiming the Heart of a Duke

Intriguing the Viscount

Giving a Heart of Lace (a prequel to Winning the Merchant Earl)

Being Lady Harriet's Hero

Enchanting the Duke (coming soon)

Redeeming the Marquess (coming soon)

Healing Lord Barton (coming soon)

Winning the Merchant Earl (coming soon)

Loving the Bitter Baron (coming soon)

Rescuing the Countess (coming soon)

Attracting the Spymaster (coming soon)

The Derbyshire Set

A Gift of Love (Prequel short story)

A Devil's Bargain (Prequel short story - coming soon)

The Earl's Unexpected Bride

The Captain's Compromised Heiress

The Viscount's Unsuitable Affair

The Count's Impetuous Seduction

The Rake's Unlikely Redemption

The Marquess' Scandalous Mistress

A Remembered Face (Bonus short story – coming soon)

The Marchioness' Second Chance (coming soon)

A Viscount's Reluctant Passion (coming soon)

Lady Theodora's Christmas Wish

The Duke's Improper Love (coming soon)

Other Books

The Scottish Governess (coming soon)

The Earl's Reluctant Fiancée (coming soon)

The Crew of the Seadragon's Soul Series, (coming soon - a set of 10 linked novels)

For everyone who had the grace to be patient while this book, and the ones before and after it, were coming into existence, who provided cups of tea, and food, when the writing would not let me go, and endured countless times being asked for opinions.

For the readers coming to know these characters well, and who inspire me to continue, by buying my books!

And for all the writers of Regency Historical Romance, whose books I read, who inspired me to write in this fascinating period.

Chapter One

Anna Perkins' hands were shaking along with the jellies on top of the tray. This was the first major occasion since she had been promoted to housemaid, and she desperately wanted to make a good impression.

The demands of a huge occasion such as this - the first large house party after the rather scandalous wedding of the houses' master, the Earl of Stanningfield, required input from every single person employed in the household, preparing the feasts and the rounds of drinks or teas that went between, keeping the house neat and orderly without disrupting the guests, and serving everything up in a tidy and efficient operation.

This was how she found herself nervously picking her way along one of the principal corridors of the main part of the house.

A part of it so grand and smart she had barely even seen in her previous role as a scullery maid. She was, despite her protests to the housekeeper and her lack of upper body strength, quaking under the weight of a platter full of jellies.

She rounded a corner and bumped straight into something remarkably solid, which turned out to be Richard Maitland. Viscount Bellham. He was striding up the corridor purposefully, away from the rest of the house guests, and walked straight into her. There was nothing she could do. Within a clattering instant, the elegant young nobleman was covered in jelly.

'Good grief!' he was just in the process of saying, making a rudimentary effort to scrape the stuff off his jacket, when their eyes met for the first time. Anna had not had the chance to see many of the guests as yet, and certainly hadn't spoken to any. It had not been her place to look out for handsome young gentlemen, but if it had been, Viscount Bellham would have been the first she noticed.

He was tall and well-built, filling out the superbly tailored and arranged clothes she had just spilled red and yellow fruit jellies all over. He wore a rich golden waistcoat over a glistening white shirt, with an elaborate cravat, in the manner fashionable in London society, and an elegant dress coat in navy blue. His stance and posture belied an easy confidence, a swagger even. He moved forcefully, as if he always had somewhere important to be, significant things to be getting on with, and would not allow any man, woman or beast to detain him in his endeavours. His breeches clung tight to his well-formed calves and thighs, bringing tight definition to his muscular masculinity.

He had a wild look in his eyes, like a celtic druid or a warrior king, a face encircled by dark, compelling shadows, full red lips and a robust jawline. Atop his head was a beautifully coiffured mane of a rich, golden brown. As she stood beside him, her eyes meeting his, ashamed in an instant of her low status and her error with the jellies, Anna felt quite plain in her servants' uniform, and yet he seemed to be peering deep into her soul, communing with her, in some profound, impossible way, via their two sets of eyes.

His face quickly turned from angry disbelief to soft contemplation of the woman in front of him. She was completely fascinated by this man, whom she knew she could never hope to know more of than she saw in this instant, and wanted, for some reason that she did not understand, to reveal all of herself to him.

'Richard! What is going on!' the voice came from a young woman, Lady Duckington, one of the few aristocrats present whom Anna had had any contact with.

She had requested, yesterday, whilst taking tea in the drawing room, that Anna pick up a handkerchief for her. Anna had obliged, but Lady Duckington had not said even a word of thanks. Anna supposed it was to be expected - most of these upper-class ladies took their own servants entirely for granted, let alone those of other households.

She was a very attractive lady, quite beautiful to look at and extremely well-dressed and well-bred, but she had a coldness of manner that made Anna find her immediately hard to like. Her voice was piercing and harsh, like a January frost.

"Are we going to take this walk in the grounds, or aren't we…" her voice tailed off as she saw the scene before her. She did not bother to disguise her disgust. Ladies of her station could afford to be disgusted at servants, especially when they were, as Anna seemed to be here, in error. Richard, covered in sweet-smelling slime, turned to face her, breaking eye contact with Anna for the first time in what felt like ages.

"It's quite alright, Lady Duckington," he said, in a warm voice that almost glowed with its own attractiveness "I've merely had a little altercation with a tray of jellies". Without a second for pause or thought, rage spread across Lady Duckington's face.

"What in God's name did you think you were doing?!" she exclaimed, partly at Richard, mostly at Anna. "Idiotic girl! Can you people not even carry jellies correctly?"

"I'm very sorry, my Lady" said Anna, trying to curtsy, blushing with embarrassment, as a sense of desperation rose in her.

"Sorry? You're sorry, are you? Do you have any idea what this gentleman's dress coat cost, or how long the labour of the tailors on Saville Row? I expect you have no idea, but it would be more than thrice your paltry salary! I've a good mind to summon my manservant and have you soundly thrashed in front of us, insolent girl!"

"It's quite alright, my lady" said Richard at last, intervening, to Anna's shock, on her behalf. He remained calm, even in the face of Lady Duckington's mad fury. Anna, feeling more ashamed and exposed than perhaps she ever had before, was filled with a sudden gratitude towards this man.

Would he speak on her behalf? Was he coming to her defence, her, Anna Perkins, the most junior housemaid at Havisham Hall?

"The fault was entirely mine. I have this unfortunate tendency to not look where I am going in great houses, and to stride around foolishly as if the place is my own. It must come from my father, do not blame this poor girl for my error, it is most unseemly"

"Unseemly?" Lady Duckington all but spat, her fair, round face colouring with her anger, the red of her cheeks clashing horribly with her intricately coiffed golden hair. Anna could not help but think that the Lady brought dishonour to her title by behaving like this and that her fine garments perhaps clothed a character not so fine, but could never have articulated such an insubordinate thought.

"What is truly unseemly Mr. Maitland, is that you, nephew to the Earl of Wiltshire and heir to one of the finest estates in England, should have your best clothes drenched in jelly, and then feel a strange desire to speak in defence of a low-born servant! I ask you! You can quite forget about that walk around the grounds! I'm off to seek out the company of someone a little less..." she looked him up and down in disgust. Her face seemed oddly well-used to contorting itself into contemptuous glares "...eccentric". With that she was off, leaving the two of them alone. Maitland turned to face Anna, smiling, a laugh forming at the back of his throat.

"She isn't always like that" he said, seeing the funny side of the entire situation. "On occasion she can even be quite charming. On occasion that is..."

"Oh sir!" Anna said, stepping forward in desperation and trying, almost without thinking, to soften her country girl's accent, in the presence of this prominent gentleman. "Words cannot express how sorry I am! I thank you kindly for accepting some measure of blame in front of Lady Duckington, but really the fault was all mine, however can I make it up to you?" she realised that in her unguarded moment, compelled by some intense attraction swelling inside her, she had reached out to take one of his hands. Rather than pulling away and chastising her for this completely inappropriate action, Maitland threw her a dark smile, wry and fascinating.

"Well you can start by ceasing this ridiculous grovelling" he said lightly. She drew back, fearing at once that she had made herself foolish and vulnerable before him.

"- and then when you are quite restored to your senses, you can accompany me to my quarters to help me change into something slightly less..." he sniffed his coat, glistening with the spilled jelly. "- fragrant." Despite herself, she giggled a little at his remark, and they set off together up the main staircase of Havisham Hall towards the guest suites.

As befit a man of his status, and his friendship with Charles Rockingham, Earl of Stanningfield and master of this house, Richard Maitland, Viscount Bellham, was staying in one of the finest of Havisham's many chambers. It was, in many ways, a hang-over from Havisham's past, and had not been comprehensively refurbished by the new Earl in a fashionable, modern way, like so much of the front of the house.

A seemingly ancient four-poster bed dominated the room, carved, back in the 16th century, in rich mahogany and draped in tapestry hangings, which had faded a little with time, but upon which the finely stitched scenes of hunting and feasting were still visible. Only one of the walls had been re-plastered and painted in a light shade, as had much of the rest of the house, to give it a sense of airy lightness, the rest remained wood panelled, with a heavy, stately air.

There were two landscape paintings facing each other on the west and east walls, an enormous wardrobe and dresser, and the stuffed head of a small deer, shot by the previous Earl, mounted next to the bed. The whole room conveyed a certain antique luxury. Anna did not think she had ever been in this particular room before.

"Ghastly bedchamber really" said Richard as they entered. "I've no idea why Stanningfield is always so keen to put me up in here, although, I suppose, having never complained, I can only really blame myself".

"The room seems quite wonderful to me sir" she said, still awestruck by its grandeur.

"Yes, I can see why it might, but I can't abide all this old stuff" he replied briskly, tapping at the varnished oak panelling around the walls.

"Don't really like sharing my sleeping space with that old boy, either" he gestured at the deer's head "- but then I suppose it wouldn't be an English country house without some severed animal parts. We of the gentry have a certain image to keep up, don't we?"

Anna had no idea what to say in response to all of this upper-class irony. She was gaining insights here that she had never thought she would get, glimpsing a world that had not ever been her own. It was overwhelming and fascinating in equal measure.

"What is your name, girl?" he turned to face her again. The fine hairs on her arms lifted, and a jolt of nervous energy ran through her the instant their eyes met.

"I hope I have not bored you into submission with all my talk of great houses?"

"No sir, not a bit"

"Good. Then you won't mind me asking what your name is?"

"Of course not sir, it is Anna Perkins" she said it with a curtsey and a practiced look of innocence and modesty. It was good for servants to pretend that they had no personality at all, when they spoke to the upper classes. As far as their employers' were concerned, they were there to fulfil their duty and nothing more. She thought to add, unnecessarily: "a simple name, for nought but a simple housemaid."

"Not a bit! It is quite a charming name, in its own way. You need not assume all of us gentle-folk have no interest in our servants as people" he was coming closer to her now. She tried to contain the nervous, quivering sensations inside her, as he came so close that she could almost feel his breath mingling with hers.

"We're not all like Lady Amelia Duckington, thank Christ!" he laughed, and she smiled at him nervously, unsure where she stood.

Softly, gently, his finger stroked her chin, tilting her face closer to his. She was struck by surprise, unsure how to respond to this man, who actually saw her as a person, but at the same time a huge part of her knew that she desired this, desired him. She consented to his touch, allowed him to move her as he wished, enjoying the sensation of his hand on her as he ran his fingers across her skin, silently encouraging it.

"You are a rather fair young lady, Miss Perkins" he said. She instinctively looked away, concealing the redness spreading across her face at this unexpected compliment. "I am disappointed that I did not have the chance to make your acquaintance sooner."

Then, in a single movement he turned away from her, and gestured down at his clothes, still covered in the sticky evidence of their earlier run-in. The jelly was already beginning to smell quite strongly, as the heat of his body warmed it through his clothes, thought the practical-minded servant in Anna.

"Come, help me out of these clothes. You cannot deny it; you played some part in their ruin, you can assist me in their salvation."

"Of course sir!" she said, hurrying over to him at once. He had all but taken his coat off himself, but the jelly had spilled all over the rest of his clothes as well, from his collar, right down to his breeches.

Despite her lack of experience with gentleman's clothing, and the fact that she knew that really Viscount Bellham ought to have summoned his valet to perform this duty, and therefore might only have employed her to assist him with some salacious intent, she began at once to undress him.

It was most rash of her to do so, but in his presence she seemed to have lost all caution.

Her nimble fingers worked at his cravat, untying the elaborate knot that had no doubt taken quite some time to tie to its perfect, fashionable state, and then easing it away from his neck.

She was forced to press herself very close to him to do this, their faces almost touching.

The temptation to steal an upwards glance at his face was, at one stage, too much but she noted, with more than a hint of disappointment, he was staring imperiously into the middle distance, aloof, clearly used to the attention of servants in this manner.

She then began to loosen the buttons on his waistcoat. The tight definition of the muscles in his chest and abdominal region was clearly visible beneath his well fitted shirt, and she felt a strong desire to run her fingers over the cloth, to feel that hard warmth beneath her hand.

She resisted the temptation.

The more of his clothes she removed, the more she felt a swelling inside her, a heat rising from her lower body, a desire to feel him, and for him to feel her. It was more than a year now, since John had been killed in the war, and she had not been with a man since, nor wanted to be. Until now.

The demands of her position, the need for her to keep at her duties and perform as required, to in no way act above her station, made these sensations all the more acute – how utterly impossible of her, to want a man like this, a Viscount!

Finally, the waistcoat removed, he pulled his shirt over his head and, tossing it carelessly aside for his valet to clean up later, he turned to face her, shirtless, standing tall and proud, awaiting the attention of her hands on his breeches. She took a deep breath, and considered backing out of this situation, fleeing the room, but instead, found herself stepping forward.

"… with sir's permission" she said, as impassively as she could manage.

"Granted, of course" he said, with a grin. She nodded, and began to delicately undo the buttons of his falls, her breathing coming harder as she did so.

What would it be like, to run her hands over his hips, to touch his manhood, to bring him to full arousal, to sate her desire with him ?

She pushed the thoughts aside, and focused only on easing down his breeches, over those tempting hips, in such a way as to avoid smearing jelly on his skin. Once the breeches reached his knees, he sat, with care not to spread jelly onto the brocade of the chair, and waited for her to pull of his boots.

She did so, with her eyes carefully averted, no matter how much she wished to look, as nothing now preserved his modesty. The boots removed, with a final, faltering pull she slid the breeches from his feet and cast them aside to join the shirt.

Turning back she was met immediately with the sight of a throbbing, pulsing manhood, turgid and magnificent. Her nipples hardened, and a pulse of hot need shot between her legs. It had been so long!

"I appear to be rather exposed" he said, still smiling. "I was not expecting so close an inspection of my intimate areas."

"Sir…" she could not think what to say in response, but she did not have to. Before she could utter another word their mouths met and he was kissing her, with demanding passionate lips, penetrating her mouth with a tongue as stiff and proud as the instrument between his legs.

The heat of intense desire pulsed in both of them, a shared need making them lean into each other, his strong arms wrapping around her.

She was overcome with sensation, with the memories of how good it could be between a man and a woman.

Her desire rushed through her body, making her mouth even more heated on his and the wetness of her intimate flesh spread against her simple servant's petticoats. Could this really be happening, here, with the nephew of the Earl of Wiltshire?

It was. Unlikely as it seemed, this was really happening to her, sensations overwhelming her, desire rushing through her in waves as their tongues jostled and jousted, tangling together in their mouths.

He stroked her body lightly, ran his hand over her breasts and nipples, where they stood proud against the thin fabric of her worn servant's dress, sending great tremors of desire all through her. Her entire being seemed to be in thrall to him, she could feel every hair on her body standing on edge, her skin prickling at his touch, sense forces greater than either of them pulsing through their two bodies, compelling them together.

She seemed to lose herself in his embrace, strong, firm, warm, the room around her, with all its panelling and decoration, fading away into a blur.

Sensation was all there was, and she ceased to consciously be aware of where they were or who they were. In that moment, he ceased to be Richard Maitland, Viscount Bellham, and became only a beautiful man, naked in sensual communion, with her, a woman, clothed.

They would have made a rather odd sight had anyone had cause to enter what had turned from a sombre bedchamber into a dangerous boudoir, but Anna was too caught up in his kiss to think such trivial thoughts. The world outside meant nothing in comparison to this sensation, this intensity.

She felt his hands straying, delicately but with a certain force, down towards her most vulnerable area. He worked his way under the outer façade of the drab dress, into the plain and practical underclothes, towards that area which promised so much to both man and woman, and which was now throbbing and beating in time with her racing heart.

His hand brushed aside her modesty and felt the wetness down there, the little bundle of hair above her aching femininity, and he groaned against her mouth. Then slowly, deliberately, he eased a finger into her, so that she bucked her hips against his hand and whimpered her pleasure at the sensation. He nibbled and kissed on her neck as he did this, biting her softly, more delicate and arousing than she had thought possible, in a way that she was not used to but immediately liked.

She was prepared to give herself to him, to feel more than just his hand in her, her desire overriding any concerns that she may have felt, but then he stopped. She rocked on her feet, unsteady and confused as he pulled his hand out from beneath her skirts, and stepped back, almost embarrassed. He gave her a little kiss on the top of her head, and turned away.

"I'm sorry. We should not do this."

"What? Why?" she said, momentarily forgetting her station, and the scandalous nature of this encounter.

He had no way to know that she was a widow, that she knew what went on between men and women, and might desire this for herself.

"I did not wish to take advantage of you in this manner. I apologise. I should have summoned my valet for this task. I shall attend to changing my attire in my own turn." He looked at her with a compelling compassion wrought across his face. He seemed oddly vulnerable there, completely naked and looking at her with sympathy.

She felt strange. A huge part of her simply wanted this handsome gentleman to grab her and ravish her and share the pleasures that she knew they both wanted.

But on the other hand, it was right that he had done this. She was perhaps more worldly than he assumed, but his concern for her honour and her welfare was flattering. He started to move towards his wardrobe.

"Before you leave however, it would be remiss of me not to make use of the practised and no doubt tasteful eye of a young lady in assisting me with selecting my attire."

He beckoned her over, throwing the wardrobe open to reveal several ranks of finely tailored shirts and coats, and beautifully pressed breeches. She was entranced by them, the range of colours and cuts greater than any she had ever imagined possible.

"How do you feel Viscount Bellham should dress himself?" he said, squeezing her hand lightly and smiling at her. She looked up, still in awe.

There was such a broad selection here that she was not at all surprised that he wanted a second opinion. It was unusual indeed for her to get such an intimate insight into a man's private life, especially a man of such breeding and distinction, and she rather liked it.

Glancing across the many options in front of her, her eye, and her small servant's hand, came to rest on the sleeve of a charming jacket in a sky blue.

"With sir's permission?"

"Granted, of course"

"Though little versed in the arts of men's tailoring, I feel that this one would suit sir's complexion and hair very handsomely."

"Yes, yes I think you might be right" he said, taking the jacket from the wardrobe.

"I usually have my man Thompson take care of such sartorial questions, but I can see that you have quite an eye for clothing."

She blushed at the compliment. As he held the jacket up against his muscled torso, she could see that she was not wrong. The light colour of the jacket seemed only to lend the dark, enchanting richness of the Viscount's eyes an extra glimmer.

"Perhaps in concert with a fine cream shirt and cravat, and darker buff breeches?"

"Certainly sir, an excellent selection."

"Very good, very good" he said, gathering the necessary clothes. "I feel it would be best if I dressed myself now, my servants would be most confused were I to summon them at this juncture and they were to walk in on me unclothed. I have little experience of these things but I shall do my best to make myself presentable."

She laughed at this. It had never entirely occurred to her just how much gentlefolk depended on their servants, but now she was confronted with the notion it made perfect sense. To think that this fully-grown young man, intelligent, fit and lively, had little idea of how to dress himself in the morning without the assistance of another! She giggled inwardly, imaging him struggling with his button holes and fumbling at the edges of his cravat. How ridiculous the upper classes were, up close and behind closed doors!

Her thoughts drew a smile to her face, causing him to exclaim, wryly "I can see that you find my predicament amusing" as he pulled on his undershirt.

"I suppose it is to a more practical minded person. We nobles really would be quite lost without our servants, we depend upon you entirely."

She laughed again, this time out loud. His self-awareness was very attractive. He was neither a snob nor a prude, but merely a man who happened to have a lot of money and a good family. She felt even more drawn to him, and she hoped, he to her.

"You'd best leave now, we don't want to generate any unnecessary gossip.

You should hear some of the mother hens Stanningfield invited to this party, they have nothing better to do than whisper to each other about scandals concerning people they barely know. I could not stand to give them any more fodder. Good day, Miss. Perkins" and he leant in and kissed her softly and affectionately on the cheek. Anna left the room, struggling to repress the urge to turn around and beam at him, feeling like an entirely new person.

Chapter Three

Edward Greenidge was a scholar, and it was his opinion that large balls, house parties and the like were no place for scholars. It was not that he did not like the company, or that he considered it to be in some way alien to him.

He was here for the same reasons as everyone else of course, on account of his ties to the great and noble families who were here to enjoy the Earl of Stanningfield's hospitality, and to get a closer look at the woman whom he had married, in that rather delightfully scandalous wedding.

Like everyone else, he had been at first shocked, and then stunned into silence, and then finally delighted at the wedding ceremony itself, when the Earl had spurned his pre-arranged dynastic match, to the Earl of Derbyshire's daughter, for the love of a humble governess.

Along with all the others, he had spoken about nothing else now for two whole days. It was like a fever that had come over the entire party, and the only way to sweat it out seemed to be through constant gossip and speculation.

"Well of course this will be the ruin of the Stanningfield name" one Lady had said. Greenidge could not now recall her first name, if he had even bothered to learn it. Such trivialities did not concern him, but what was of interest to a scholar of the Royal College of Arms had been her title and position. She was the wife of Phillip Grey, Marquess of Tewkesbury, and that made her by marriage (he recalled instantly from memory) the great, great, great, great, great, great sister-in-law of Sir Thomas Fairfax, victor of Marston Moor and Naseby. These were the sorts of details that did exercise his academic imagination.

"I wouldn't be quite so sure" another lady, the Dowager Baroness of Wycombe, had said. "Loath as I am to repeat idle servant's gossip, I have heard that Lord Stanningfield's new bride is in fact a descendent of the de Quincys." Greenidge's ears had immediately pricked up at this. He believed he may have slurped his tea, drawing disapproving looks from the great ladies nearby, but this did not concern him. A descendant of the de Quincy line was quite a discovery! They were one of the oldest lost houses of England, one of the great medieval dynasties, and the thought of them being revived through a love marriage was remarkable enough to exercise his imagination. Perhaps he could investigate the subject further, possibly put a little treatise together for the college?

"Even if that is the case, no good will come of it" the first woman had said. "Even if she is a de Quincey, they are a spent force. They have no money, no estates, their title is quite meaningless."

"Meaningless?" Greenidge had cut in, surprising all and sundry. "I think not, er, er, er, even without any tangible claim to er, er, as you, say, monies, er, lands, er, er, houses, etc. er, the name of de Quincy should not be considered a trifle. Why they were er, er, one of the greatest of the Norman houses, er, er, on a par with say, er, the de Montforts, who have the focus of much of my later, er, er, er, research as you might put it, and…" but the ladies, little interested in what the renowned man of letters had to say, had cut him off and carried on their gossip.

Such social occasions had never really been the scholar's natural habitat, and he was quite used to such indifference. Now, bored with the company and used to the guests' lack of interest in his insights on questions of inheritance and titles, he was making his way off to the library, confident that there he would find diversion more to his liking.

The library was certainly a splendid room, fit for a great house like Havisham. From what Greenidge knew of the Earl, he suspected that its master was not much of a reading man, but whether he had assembled this collection of books and manuscripts for his own purposes, merely for showing off to guests, or if he had come into them via some other means (presumably inheritance) did not matter. The Earl's excellent collection covered a wide range of topics, and included a few rare volumes that he absolutely must read whilst here.

Organised over more than a dozen huge shelves, all of them stretching from floor to ceiling, every type of book under the sun seemed to be present, from the ancient classics to modern texts on science and philosophy, via books of medieval and Tudor poetry and plays, and even a variety of different novels.

The escritoire on the far wall commanded excellent views of the grounds via one of the defining features of this house, the tall windows, so clear and well-wrought that, at first glance, they seemed open, looking out towards a spinney of trees the other side of a meadow, laid out discreetly in the English fashion. Greenidge lost all sense of time, wandering slowly around the perimeter of the room, glancing at the titles, making his selection.

He was filled with the same feeling he always felt when confronted with a well-stocked library - an erratic desire somehow to read all of the hundreds of books here, all at once, and soak in the knowledge that they held as rapidly as he could.

Despite being the third son of a Viscount, ordinary aristocratic pursuits had never interested him much. Hunting was tiresome, shooting rather over-stimulating, gambling a waste of money, parties and balls a bore, riding and driving fast frightening and fishing a total waste of everyone's time. Ever since he was a small boy all he'd wanted to do was find a quiet corner in which to read, and, as a professor of the Royal College of Arms, that is how he spent his days. He was rather proud of having found a solution to being a third son, which did not involve going into either the army or the clergy.

Noting with pleasure that the books were arranged by genre and type, he made his way over to the section on the history of the heraldry of the nobility, his favourite subject. Pulling a book with an intriguing title, *Arms and Mottos of Angevin England,* by one Harold Jenkinson, from the shelf, he sat down in a plump leather armchair and began to read.

However, just as Greenidge was settling in to absorbing the wisdom held therein, he was disturbed by the sound of a servant entering with a feather duster. He did not know it just yet, but the girl in her modest black uniform was Anna Perkins.

"Oh, hello there!" he said at once, startling her for a second with his sudden speech. "I'm afraid you've er, er quite caught me! I slipped away from the, er, main body of the party as it were to make a, er, er, er, perusal of some of the volumes. A most interesting selection you have here at Havisham, it must be said!"

"Begging your pardon sir, I didn't realise there was anyone here." Anna curtsied automatically, doing everything that she could to conceal the flushes that were still running all up and down her body from her earlier encounter with Viscount Bellham. "I shall leave you in peace."

"No, no! No need for that, don't be silly, girl!" Greenidge replied. Despite his eccentricity, and clear dis-ease in the company of people, as opposed to books, he had a warm and open manner that Anna took an immediate liking to. Unlike so many of the snooty toffs present at the wedding celebration she thought, this old chap seems to be genuine, good-natured and honest in his intentions.

"I would not wish to er, er, disrupt your no doubt vital domestic duties! A house like this must require daily labour, do what er, er, you will."

"Thank you sir, that is most kind of you." Anna smiled, turning to carry on her with her dusting. She noted, as well, a selection of used china tea cups on one of the tables that would need to be cleared away. Evidently this fellow was not the first to be attracted to the tranquil atmosphere of the library, away from the other guests.

"I'm so sorry!" Greenidge added suddenly "- where on earth have I left my manners today, er, permit me to introduce myself, Professor Edward Greenidge, er, er, scholar-resident at the Royal College of Arms in London." Anna turned and curtsied again.

"A pleasure to make your acquaintance, Professor" she said, hoping that she had used the correct term of address. She had never met a professor before. This role as housemaid certainly beat slaving away down in the pantry and kitchens! She seemed to be meeting all manner of interesting gentle folk. "Wait 'til folk back down in Harteston hear about all this!" she thought.

"As a scholar of heraldry and familial ancestry, I make it er, er, my habit to ask the names of all those who's acquaintance I, er, make. Tell me, girl, what is your full name?"

"Why it is Anna Jane Perkins, sir. That's my married name – my husband's dead, like so many others in the war. Anna Jane Winton is what I was christened as, if you'll pardon me, er, Professor."

"Oh yes, yes absolutely!" he replied, seeming oddly enthused all of a sudden. He was so enthused in fact, that he rose to his feet and seemed about to start pacing contemplatively. He then turned to her in an instant, with a serious, startled look on his face. Anna was worried that she had made some accidental digression and offended this scholar, and was about to start apologising profusely when he began speaking again.

"I'm sorry, did you say Perkins, by any chance?" he said with a new energy, his usual stammer completely forgotten.

"Yes sir, I did. It was my husband's surname, if you take me correctly."

"I do, I most certainly do!" he said forcefully, almost seeming to jump into the air. "And you are a native of this fair county, born and raised in one of the villages proximate to this house?"

"Most certainly, professor. I've lived my whole life in Harteston parish, as far as I am aware. All of the records are, I believe, in order down at the church registry. My husband was born and raised here too." She could not quite understand his interest. Why was he scrutinizing her like this?

"Tell me" continued Professor Greenidge, serious all over again "- did your husband have a father by the, er, forgive me, rather unusual Christian name of Franklin?" Anna was astounded. In fact she was suddenly a little frightened, and began to back away from this strange man of letters.

"Why, yes sir, he did". She confirmed, trying to conceal how startled she was. "That was my husband's father's name, all of his life."

"Most interesting." Greenidge muttered to himself, his manic energy subsiding as he returned to his book. "Most interesting indeed. You will forgive me, Miss Perkins, I will detain you from your er, er, er, duties, no further. I have er, ample reading to be getting on with. But er, thank you er, er, most kindly for your co-operation in my little er, er, cross-examination." He stuck his nose firmly back into the book, and left Anna, confused and a little worried for the clever fellow's sanity, to carry on with her allotted chores.

Chapter Four

Only a few short hours after finishing her duties in the library (ignoring the muttering and somewhat frantic reading habits of Professor Greenidge as best she could), Anna was back in the pantry receiving orders from the housekeeper, Mrs. Cartwright. She was a stern and doughty woman who seemed at times to be running Lord Stanningfield's household like a military camp. Her twenty-something years of dedicated service had made her fiercely loyal to her lord and employer, and she didn't care who knew it:

"Ah Miss Perkins!" she boomed as Anna slipped in, hoping in vain not to be noticed by her superiors.

"I have about your little encounter with Viscount Bellham in the west wing! You ought to bloody well look where you're going, lass!"

Anna was immediately conscious that her face might be turning red at this mention of the Viscount. Certainly her heart fluttered uncontrollably, in a way she was not used to. The flush of infatuation immediately turned to anxious panic though, when she thought about exactly what Mrs. Cartwright might have heard.

Could she possibly have heard about her accompanying him to his own private quarters, and what had transpired after that?

"If you don't wish to be demoted back down to scullery maid you'll mind where you're going! There's plenty of little nooks and crannies and blind corners about this great house, and it's your duty as a servant to see that you don't disrupt the activities of Lord Stanningfield's guests, not the other way around. See that you are more discreet in future!"

"Yes, ma'am" Anna said, demurely. Part of her wanted to object, to complain that it had not been her who'd come running around the corner of a corridor in an unfamiliar house, pursued by someone she was not married to, but she held her tongue.

She knew what her job was worth, relative to questions of truth and justice.

As a servant, it was often best just to put up and shut up. And, as it seemed that Mrs Cartwright had heard nothing more than that there had been an unfortunate collision, involving the tray of jellies, she was certainly not going to do anything to encourage further questions! She took a deep relieved breath, and waited to see what came next.

'Now my dear' continued Mrs. Cartwright, warmer and more affectionate all of a sudden.

"Upstairs, in the principle drawing room, many of the guests are taking another round of tea. Not my place to question how much of the stuff these ladies and gentlemen like to drink, though you may have noted, it is rather a lot. Here..." she gestured to a few platters assembled on a simple wooden table "- are some additional refreshments, cakes, scones, fondant fancies and the like. See that they reach their intended recipients unspoiled this time, and you shall find your way back into my good books".

Anna nodded purposefully, in the way one gets used to doing as a servant, and, taking two platters of little cakes in her arms, started up the stairs towards the main body of the party, and, though she did not know it yet, but already sincerely hoped, towards Viscount Bellham.

Unfortunately, from her perspective, the first person that Anna came to as she entered the sumptuous drawing room of Havisham Hall was Lady Duckington. As usual she appeared to be avoiding the company of her husband, who was more than twice her age, in favour of a gaggle of admiring upper-class girls, most of them plain and unwed, who seemed to cling to the hems of her richly tailored dresses like children.

Lady Duckington was just holding forth as Anna quietly picked her way over to them:

"Of course the Haymarket theatre isn't anything like as good as it used to be" she pronounced in her arrogant manner, all eyes fixed on her.

"I saw a marvellous production of *Julius Caesar* there when I was but a girl, and it was the first time I really fell in love with the theatre, do you remember that, the first great awakening of a love of the stage?" her onlookers all nodded as one, sycophantically.

"But since then the place has become a complete and utter dump. I mean no-one who is anyone in London society would be seen dead in the place these days. They turn out a lot of rot- Gay, and Bacon and all of those absurd little fellows - and employ some of the most disreputable players this side of Samarkand to boot. As I say, no-one with any sense of taste or decency would be seen dead in the place."

Anna slipped in among the assembled young ladies, and started delicately placing cakes on their saucers.

The intention was to do so without being noticed at all, as if to maintain an illusion for the nobility that servants and working people did not in fact exist, and that their tea and cakes and meals all appeared out of thin air. Unfortunately, being still quite new to the domestic arts, she did not seem to have succeeded:

"I say girl!" Lady Duckington said to her directly, in a manner unbecoming to anyone, let alone a lady of her standing.

"Are you the coarse little servant who spilled jellies all over Viscount Bellham earlier?"

Anna looked up. She stammered. What should she say? Ideally she ought to say nothing, but when engaged directly in this rather unorthodox manner, by a guest, she had to respond somehow.

Yet she could not seem to get her lips or tongue to work, and she had a strange, sticky feeling already at the back of her throat, as if someone had poured glue down it to prevent her from ever speaking again.

"You are aren't you?" Lady Duckington said, with a malicious glint in her eyes. Her admirers tittered pathetically along.

"You are that idiot girl who ruined the Viscount's finest dress coat! I'm surprised they kept you on at all after that, you people have one, simple job to do and you botched it entirely! You ought to go back to pulling pints for farmhands! Present company is far too good for you!" The company laughed again, with Lady Duckington, at Anna.

The poor serving girl carried on with her duties, laying the little cakes down as diligently as she could, but she felt an overwhelming urge to run away, and cry, and never come back to Havisham Hall, or these cruel noble folk, who assumed that they were better than her, just because they had titles, money and big houses!

Oh if only she were a Lady and could give this stuck-up madam a piece of her mind, but she was only the daughter of simple James Winton, the ploughman, and wife, once, of plain Franklin Perkins, and it was not her place to share her thoughts with the great and the good.

"And whilst I have your ear..." Lady Duckington was relentless! She could not help herself, some horrible instinct deep inside her seemed to compel her to be cruel! *What on earth was wrong with her?* a more self-assured person might have allowed themselves to think.

"I have to ask you, maid, why the dreadful quality of cakes in this house? I had thought better of Lord Stanningfield quite frankly, his staff appear to be nothing but clumsy dullards and dribbling village morons!"

Her followers seemed very amused by this latest quip, falling about in laughter as they crammed cake into their over-privileged mouths. Anna was quietly seething, and was about to draw away from them, towards what she hoped would be a kinder party on the other side of the room.

"Why only the other day I had a fondant fancy that was harder and staler than the Rock of Gibraltar!" She drew more laughter, but it was suddenly silenced by a new arrival, a different presence on the edge of the conversation.

All at once the silly unmarried girls stopped their laughing, remembered to cover their mouths as their nannies had taught them, and looked up at the handsome bachelor who had stepped, without a moment's pause, into their conversational circle.

Anna looked up from her platter to see the Viscount, looking right at her, with a warm smile on his face, still wearing the same sky blue coat and cream cravat she had helped him into earlier.

"Are you harassing the staff, Lady Duckington?" he said boldly, in a light-hearted tone that took all of the malice out of the situation at once. "Come, come, this poor girl has had more than enough grief from me over her earlier error, haven't you Anna? She needs no further reminder of her simple mistake, it could have happened to any of us."

"Any of us who are forced to carry trays around for a living!" Lady Duckington said, her sadistic wit muted a little by the Viscount's presence. "Some of us have the means and breeding to avoid so lowly a fate!"

"Indeed, but we would do well to demonstrate that breeding better by treating our spiritual equals with a little kindness." he gazed into Anna's eyes with an intensity she had never seen in any gentleman before.

He had come to her defence, this charming young gentleman! She was astounded, and felt a renewed desire for him, as acute as it had been before, barely suppressed beneath her serving girls' attire.

"Without staff, we of the gentry are nothing, and we would do well to remember that. As to the quality of Havisham's fondant fancies..." he said, cheekily plucking a cake from Lady Duckington's saucer and taking a bite.

"- I fancy that Miss Perkins here is not responsible for such matters, and that their fondancy, along with their freshness has been dimmed somewhat by the length of our stay as guests. I expect that the household has good reason to wish for our swift departure back to our estates so that they who actually know a little of baking and hospitality may return to a less hard-pressed mode of existence. You will excuse me..."

And with that he left the company to sip their tea and nibble their cakes in stunned silence, quite trumped by his logic.

As he passed by Anna, he slipped a small note into the front of her pinafore in a single, deft movement, threw her a warm and friendly wink, and passed on out of the room to attend to his own business.

Anna continued her duties glowing inside, concealing her blush and fairly throbbing with her new desires.

By the time Anna had finished serving up her cakes, her entire body was fairly swollen with excitement and anticipation. The note sat in her pinafore, exercising her imagination, compelling her attention. She could not help but glance down at it a few times; the humble piece of crumpled parchment that she had already invested with so much wonder and hope, the vessel bearing her into what she prayed would be a better, happier future.

What could he possibly have to say to her, the young noble who had just come to her defence in the presence of his peers? She did not, and could not, possibly know, until she had opened it up and read it, and she could not do that until she had served all the cakes, as she was required to.

Despite her trembling hand and blushing, sweaty brow, she went about her duty as diligently as she could, until she could finally get away, return the platters to the kitchen, sneak into the storage rooms a minute, and read what he had written to her.

The note was small and brief, but it was written in a flowing, elegant script. She immediately noted the excellence of his handwriting, so much finer than her own. She was grateful as well, for her simple village schooling, received as part of the bequest of Harteston Parish and the charity of the local gentry, a privilege not afforded to many ploughmen's daughters in the Kingdom of England. Anna had always been very proud of her ability to read, being, to her knowledge, the first member of her family to be at all literate. She was a little shaky, especially on bigger words, but she could read and write well enough to get by. It had helped her to secure this job at Havisham hall, in fact, and she employed the skill now, for a letter addressed exclusively to her:

My dear Anna,

I must confess I enjoyed our earlier interaction a great deal. It would be pleasant to see more of you, and converse further, if your duties permit it. If you possibly can, meet me in the grounds in one hour, at six o'clock. I will be by the entrance to the maze.

Yours, B.

He had given away little, but it was more than enough to pique her interest. So he had enjoyed their earlier interaction! She was overwhelmed by the thought. It had been her fear, that she had tried to push to the back of her mind but which was large and persistent enough to worry her considerably in the hours since, that he had simply used her as an easy-going, immediately to hand, relief for his masculine desires, as she knew many hot-headed young gentlemen, who were yet to settle down with a bride, often did with serving girls.

He had said that she was pretty, and she had heard it often enough in the past to suspect that he meant it, but for him to take an interest in more than just her body was deeply flattering and filled her with hope and joy. She thought back to their earlier closeness, to the touch of his skin and his firm, muscular frame, his erect manhood and clean-cut jaw. The thought of him filled her and she overflowed with happiness, and with desire.

She forced herself into caution however. They had not fully consummated their earlier interaction, and Anna knew enough of such matters to suspect that he would desire more of her. In his mind, most likely, it would be her who would be revealing her naked body and most intimate anatomical features to him, and, despite her attraction, this filled her with wariness. She knew (indeed, Lady Duckington had been at great pains to remind her not ten minutes ago) that she was lowly, a country girl working in domestic service. If the Viscount did have feelings towards her he would know, even more clearly than she, that any sort of match between them would be out of the question.

And then of course, there was that other thing, her secret, which she did not dare to impart to him, or to anyone else for that matter. "I must be cautious" she thought, before looking up at the clock to see that she had already spent more than ten minutes pacing the room, in feverish contemplation of the note, and of Richard Maitland, Viscount Bellham.

She hurried from the storage room, hoping that Mrs Cartwright would not find anything more for her to do right now. She looked up as she hurried through the entrance hall, to check on the time on the grand old clock that stood there. She should not really be here at this time, but it was the most accurate clock in the house, and she wanted to be sure of the time. It was already twenty-five minutes to six, there would be no time to get ready, even had she had any other clothes or anything she wanted to do.

Anna slipped briefly into her little room in the servants' quarters. There was a little time to kill, and she knew she would have to avoid getting pulled into any more work for the present time. She sat down and had a little sip of water. As hard as she tried, she could not seem to take her mind off the situation, the impending encounter, the body of the Viscount. At last she could bear it no longer, and she hurried up a servant's passageway and out into the grounds via the gamekeeper's door, panting from her hurry, and her excitement.

Chapter Six

The maze loomed dark and complex on the horizon. Anna picked her way hurriedly across the grounds, around the rose garden where she knew her new mistress Catherine liked to walk in the day-time, past a few stout trees, one of which Miss Theodora, the Earl's niece, had fallen from and broken her arm under last summer, towards her intended destination.

As a fairly junior servant of the household, she rarely had the leisure to walk in the grounds, and was grateful for any opportunity to do so. Having grown up amongst farmers, she had a certain affinity with nature, with trees and grass and streams, although she was not used to seeing them laid out in such a neat and meticulously planned manner as they were in the grounds of great houses.

Everything conformed to some plan; it was all planted and laid out, not for profit and practicality, but for decoration. The gardens were so serene and luxuriant she could not help herself but be deeply impressed.

At first she was worried that he had not come after all. She could not see him at the entrance to the maze or on any of the benches that sat around it. This filled her with dread; what if he wasn't serious? Could this all be some kind of strange prank, the like of which she had heard upper-class young gentlemen liked to play on simple serving girls for sport? Oh what a dreadful world it was, in which men could court the affection of women beneath their station, for no reason other than the apparent pleasure of deceiving!

She had started to blame herself, lapsing into familiar but very unhelpful and negative cycles of thought. *'Silly girl'*, she, said to herself, *'to think that a man like that could be interested in you'*. The doubts built to a climax and she knew not what to think, other than to be filled with shame, until finally, she saw that it had all been for nothing, for there he was. Emerging from behind one of the hedges that formed the maze was the Viscount, smiling at her and chuckling to himself.

"You look quite startled, Miss Perkins" he said with a grin.

"Do I, sir?" Her breathing was still fast and a little ragged from having hurried. She transferred her worry momentarily over to the notion that she might have been seen from the house. If word got up to Mrs. Cartwright that she had been running about the grounds there'd be hell to pay, especially if anyone suspected what her reason for doing so was.

"Well, I suppose I am in a most hard-pressed occupation, especially on occasions like this." He looked at her contemplatively "if you don't mind me saying as much, sir."

"Not a bit, I appreciate your honesty. My own servants are constantly pretending to be entirely content with the world, even when it is clear that they are not. But come now; let us not speak of such tiresome things. I should like to see that harried look on your face replaced with a smile."

This, accompanied by the twinkle in Richard's dark eyes was enough to immediately draw a smile out of Anna. She felt at ease, all her earlier worries about serving and status, and whether or not this was all a cruel deception, floated away into nothingness. The Viscount offered his hand and she took it, and they strode into the maze with confidence, looking happily into each other's faces.

"I don't suppose you might have explored this maze before, and unlocked its secrets for yourself?" he asked.

"Oh no sir, I have never had the time. I have only been employed here less than two years, and duty rarely permits us the time to stroll about the grounds for leisure." She winced inwardly. She was still talking about domestic concerns, even though he had explicitly said she should not!

A new anxiety started to grow on her; what if she had nothing to say to this fellow? Their backgrounds were so utterly different!

"Tis a pity" he said, still in a jocular tone of voice. "If we are to find ourselves lost at the centre of Havisham maze, we shall have no idea of how to get out." she laughed nervously.

He might have a point. She had never been in a maze before.

"We have a labyrinth of this type back at the house I grew up in, at Tewkesbury" he went on.

He seemed to have a great gift for making her feel comfortable, and she felt a desire to lean into him and be held.

"I fear it is not as extensive as your Lord Stanningfield's, but it is a most amusing way to pass an afternoon." He looked at her, and seemed to tighten his grip on her hand.

Her heart beat faster at his look, and she knew that her rapid breathing made her bosom heave in a way that would draw a man's eye. She tried to make her sigh quiet "- especially in good company."

Her body stirred once more, responding to him as she had to no-one since John, and the ache of need between her legs intensified, making her whole lower body tense in awareness.

She was opening herself up to him, whether she willed it or not.

"One summer, when I was still only a boy, I ran into it alone, playing at soldiers or some other such silliness. I had confidence that having grown up walking around it with senior members of my family I would know it well, but I quickly found myself lost. I ran around frantically, tears filling my eyes, worrying, thinking awful thoughts, what if I never get out, what if I die here, things like that. I was desperate. And do you know what I did, to get out?"

"What did you do sir?"

"It seems silly really, it was so obvious, and yet it took a situation like that, and what felt like hours of worry, for the notion to even come to me; all I did was I clambered up to the top of one of the hedges and looked around. It was easy enough for a spritely young fellow, I tore my shirt a little and stained it green, but by that stage I didn't care for such concerns, I just wanted to get out. And you know, from up there" he indicated the summit of the hedges, which stood seven foot tall about their heads on all sides. "- it really is rather easy to work out where you are, and where you need to go. I remember laughing when I realised I was right by the entrance all along, I'd merely panicked and missed a simple turning. I got out and never spoke of the whole sorry affair again. Until today."

He looked at her, his face close to hers. She felt him pressing close to her, their hearts beating along as one. She knew now where she stood. She had drawn an intimate admission from him, and now it felt like there was a bond between them, of things shared only together.

"There is always a solution, Anna." The sound of her name from his lips brought a little shiver to her. "No matter what our predicament, there is always a way out, to better things." As if compelled by some force greater than either of them, they had moved closer and closer together as he spoke, until his lips brushed hers and words disappeared in a kiss.

Many of the same sensations as had assailed her that morning in his chamber came over Anna, only now, away from her duties and the possibility of being seen by onlookers, she allowed herself to embrace them.

His tongue was hot and fluid in her mouth, and she did not hesitate to meet it head on, with movements of her own, bringing the two muscles together as if in a dance. He pulled her close to him, tight against his body, her breasts pressed against his hard chest, her heart pounding against his, and they lost themselves in the kiss, consumed for a few moments by wild passion. She clung to his shirt, her fingers scraping against his finely-toned body, his arms around her, one of his legs curled past hers, bringing her to him, willing her to submit to his desires. She was all too happy to do so, feeling the truth of his desire for her in the hard ridge of his cock pressed against her, feeling her own desire spiralling through her whole body, pulsing along with her heart and with him.

A modest marble bench was just to their left. They spotted it in unison, it seemed to have been placed there just for their use, for the communion of lovers lost in the maze and in each other's contemplation. He pulled her to it, lowering himself onto the marble surface, so that she found herself suddenly atop him, with her legs spread across his hips, her skirts riding up around her, and his manhood, the splendid rod she had seen and briefly touched earlier, pressed up against her, in exactly the place that she wanted it most. The sensation of it, and of their wild kissing, was almost too much, after so long without giving herself to a man. She felt it consuming her, sending warm flushes and cold shivers to all parts of her body, narrowing her vision until all she could see were rapid glimpses of her lover, his handsome face, his well-cut coat, his strong, hard shoulders. Her head was awash with feeling and she was all too happy for it to be so.

Suddenly changing pace from the initial outpouring of feeling, in a single practised motion, he lifted her from him, and laid her back on the bench , leaning over her to kiss her again as he did so. She leaned back, her cap falling from her head, and her tangle of dark red curls escaping their pins to tangle about her shoulders. She was panting in anticipation, knowing what was to come. She was no maid or virgin, she had some idea of the affairs of the heart and body, knew what her body was capable of in circumstances such as this.

Expecting him to undo his falls, and immediately press into her, as John had always been all too keen to do, she was surprised when she felt a different sensation. This was not something she had ever felt - her petticoats and drawers had been moved aside, her skirt was at her waist, but it was not Richard's manhood that was now approaching her most intimate area, but his mouth and tongue, and she gasped at this new sensation. Her breasts hardened, as if plumped up by his lapping motions, and her moistness, that had been slowly building since they had first met at the entrance to the maze, was multiplied tenfold by the sensations that his skilled tongue was creating.

Her breath quickened to a staccato pace, keeping time with his dextrous motions and with the feeling of building ecstasy that she could not suppress. She wanted to cry out, to scream affirmatives to high heaven, to keep making love to this man forever more. And yet it was almost too much, she had no knowledge of how to cope with this intensity, nothing in her experience had prepared her for this moment.

Her eyes sealed themselves firmly off from the world, the better to enable her to drink in these incredible sensations. At some point his fingers replaced his tongue, continuing to work against her flesh, driving her desire to an ever greater pitch. She barely noticed his movement as he shifted himself back up her body, and undid the buttons at her neck.

He pulled her dress open, and exposed her breasts to his tongue, kissing down the slope of her neck, to the curves of her breasts and then around each nipple. Somehow, she realised, he had undone his falls, and she felt the brush of the velvety skin of his cock against her moistness.

The sensation was exquisite, delicious, she moaned in response, her body arching up to him, thrusting her nipple further into his mouth as her hips pushed up to welcome him in.

The moment she had been waiting for, needing so desperately, came as he entered her, hard and throbbing, so defined that she could feel every inch of his length and every subtle variation in the shape of his shaft.

He slid in, slowly, but with an elemental force, and she gasped, not frantically this time, as when he had attended to her with his tongue, but in a drawn-out breath of pleasure.

She felt how wet she was, how much her body wanted for him, as he shifted and moved, drawing gasps and little moans from her, that were ever more frequent and electrified. He thrust his full length into her and she was entirely overwhelmed.

There was so much innate sensitivity in her vital areas that every touch was a rapturous new feeling, every gyration of their hips together a fraction closer to glorious climax.

He thrust into her, at first smooth and controlled, but rapidly becoming harder and faster, as the pleasure overtook his control, until, with a cry of "sir, oh Richard, sir!" her pleasure was unleashed, harder than she had ever felt it in her life, and she was momentarily lost in the sensation, and unaware of her surroundings.

He continued, slowing a little after that moment of shared intensity, savouring his own pleasure and enjoying watching her pleasure, so unrestrained, so different from the noble ladies that he had bedded.

She was warm and welcoming around his cock, wet and tight in all the right ways and he continued languidly stimulating her with every thrust. Reaching up, she ran her fingers down his body, revelling in how it felt, as his muscles moved in time to his thrusts.

She closed her eyes firmly again and allowed feeling to ebb and flow through her, from the top of her head right into her tingling, wriggling toes. That she was lying in the dirt on the bench in the maze, covered in dust, and with a menial job to return to, all seemed irrelevant now.

This was life, being loved in a way that she had never experienced before. After a short while, he began to move faster, to thrust into her harder again, as his climax came upon him, pushing him past any care for control.

She clung to him, riding his movement until at last, with a deep cry, he pulled out of her at the last moment, spilling his seed to the ground beside them.

Languidly, she considered again, how different this man was. How much care he gave to her – to choose to make sure that there would be no unplanned child from their pleasure.

They lay there in the warm air, regaining their breath under the darkening skies, watching evening creep in beyond the clouds.

"You know, I have entirely forgotten the way out of the maze. I fear I have been rather distracted." Richard said at last, still a little breathless. She laughed, and leaned over to kiss him warmly.

"It does not matter sir, I'm sure we will find a way, as you yourself said."

"You are right of course. I could always shimmy up to the top of the hedges if needs be, I just hope a passing groundsman doesn't see me" they laughed, and shared another kiss, the movements of his tongue in her mouth a delicious warm wet echo of his cock in her body just moments before.

"There is no need to call me sir, Anna" he breathed against her mouth, his teeth nibbling her bottom lip for a lingering moment. "My name is Richard, and though my family might have titles and monies, I am but a person, an Englishman and a human, like you."

"Oh sir" she said, cradling him to her bosom. "You are too kind to me, but you know that we cannot continue as equals, it is impossible."

"I know what you say, but I hate it all the same. It is absurd, these divisions we erect between people. To think that in the eyes of many, a clever, pretty and decent young woman like you is lower than a hussy like Lady Duckington, there is no justice."

"It is not my place to comment on such concerns" said Anna, modestly. She knew that, even now, after their moment of passion, she could not risk acting in any way outside what was acceptable for her station in life.

"And therein lies so much of the problem" replied Richard, tutting.

"I am brim full of desire for you, Anna, and with affection. I sense from the nature of our encounter that you are not entirely unversed in the affairs of the flesh. This pleases me, I would not wish to have robbed a young maid of her honour. And yet, my desire for you is so strong, I did not pause to ask, to check, and I am sorry that I did not do you that courtesy."

"You are correct, sir" Anna felt suddenly embarrassed at this scrutiny of her own past. "I have lain with a man in the past. I have also..." she paused, pondered. Her feelings for him were such a powerful tide that she knew that she could not hope to resist them, and she must tell him the whole truth. It might be agony, but there was no question in her mind of deceiving him.

"- also I must confess, I have been wed before, to my childhood sweetheart, down in Harteston Parish. His name was John Perkins, and we had a child." Richard sat up, a serious look suddenly crossing his face.

Anna knew that this was a difficult admission, for him as much as for her, but she did not regret her frankness.

"Good grief Anna, I had no idea."

"Well no, I do try not to bring it up in polite conversation, and I don't wear the ring neither, the memory of it all pains me too much. He died, I'm said to say, before Sam, our little one was even born. That was over two and a half years ago now, I was barely twenty years old when he passed. He went to war, like so many others, and never came home."

Tears swelled inside her, displacing all the carnal pleasure of only moments ago. She picked herself up, put her clothing to rights, and dusted herself down.

'*Oh John!*' she thought. She'd believed at the time that she'd really loved him, the sandy haired ploughman with strong arms and bluff humour, but the Lord (and war) had taken him from her, and she had not lain with a man since, until now.

"My ma and pa take care of little Sam for the present, down in their cottage. They're still young and energetic enough to care for an infant, and they have more means than I. I help them support him with the money I make working for Lord Stanningfield, and go down to see them whenever I have a spare day."

Richard came over to her, and placed his arm about her. He was clearly taken aback by this admission, but Anna was pleased by his caring reaction. A real gentleman he was, to cradle a young widow and unwed mother to him like this, laying a little kiss on her cheek.

"I fear sir that there can never be anything more between us than a little rollicking in the dust. And as enjoyable as that of course can be, there's no good or honest future in it, as my ma might say. I am of low birth and humble profession, and I have my little Sam to look after. I would not wish to burden you with such. It would be much of a burden to any farm lad, let alone a man of your station and breeding." She had a tiny hope that he might contradict her, fling himself down on one knee and declare his desire to help her, to help Sam, to be with her and ease the pain that had encased her heart these past two years.

But she knew of course, that he would not, could not, that he had his rank and inheritance to consider, and the matches that his family were no doubt planning in high society for their eligible bachelor.

"It pains me to say this, but I fear that you are correct in your analysis of our position" he said at last, gravely. "I admit to feeling strongly for you Anna, else I would not have invited you out here with me and lain with you as I did. You inner strength and concern for your child and family moves my heart and does you great credit, but I regretfully concur, we cannot go on. Over time, our relationship would come to be no more than my use of you, exploitation of you and your body, and I will not inflict that upon you."

She sobbed, and he held her for a few moments. He was a good man the Viscount, and yet she could not help but feel that it had been a mistake, after all, to come out here and lie with him as they just had. No good could ever have come of it, she could see that now.

"Now come" he said, in a softer tone. "Let us endeavour to find a way out of this infernal maze." They shared a little chuckle, and walked arm in arm to the edge of the yew-tree maze with little difficulty. As soon as they reached the boundary they uncoupled their arms and parted, he towards the grand entrance to Havisham Hall, she back towards the little passage that led to the servants' quarters, each of them alone.

Chapter Seven

Sadness at the situation between her and Richard took a while to creep up on Anna. Over the next two days she distracted herself from her worries and pains as she had for two years, by throwing herself into her work, keeping her head down and trying to focus on other things. All of the members of staff at Havisham were still immensely busy catering to the many esteemed guests of Lord Stanningfield, serving them meals, drinks, and rounds of tea to accompany their polite conversation and various efforts at aristocratic match-making.

With so many people of wealth and taste about as well, the demands of keeping the house clean and in perfect running order were greater than ever before, and so Anna filled her days, carrying trays of cakes and sandwiches here and there, dusting and polishing the surfaces and keeping the sheen on the Stanningfield family silver and crystal ornaments.

It certainly helped her to not think of Richard too much, though she did inevitably see him around the house. They exchanged polite, and highly charged, smiles and nods, but no words were said between them.

She had a brief conversation with her employer the Earl, who cornered her in the main entrance hall as she was dusting the great clock.

"Ah, Miss Perkins" he said in his rakish brogue. Anna had always considered her lord to be a rather attractive man, despite herself, and he had frequently flirted with her in the past. "Keeping busy I see. I hear that something of an unlikely friendship has developed between you and Viscount Bellham? Something to do with a platter of spilled jellies?"

"Yes, My Lord" she said at once, concerned that he was going to reprimand her for her clumsiness, or worse, that he knew about their encounter in the maze. Would she be dismissed in disgrace? Would she have to face the notorious Stanningfield rage?

"Regrettably word has got out, but I care little for such trifles. Jelly has never been worth making any great fuss over; and Bellham has claimed sole responsibility for the incident. Decent chap, Bellham, been a good friend to me over the years." Anna bowed and nodded, not having anything to say in response.

"Just as long as you don't make a habit of depositing confectionary on my guests, I think I can turn a blind eye to this one." He gave her a little wink, demonstrating that he was only joking.

"Between you and me, I can think of a few other guests at this seemingly never-ending party of mine who might benefit from having something spilled upon them, but do not interpret that as encouragement. I've enough gossip to cope with as it is..." he rolled his eyes, alluding to his rather unusual love marriage, and with a friendly smile he left, leaving Anna feeling quite relieved.

Later the same day she had an even stranger encounter with Professor Greenidge, who was just hurrying out of his beloved library with a very purposeful look upon his face.

"Ah!" he had exclaimed, giving her a momentary turn. "Miss Perkins wasn't it?" she nodded assent, still slightly disturbed by the scholar's knowledge of her family. "I had been hoping to er, er, er, bump into you, as it, were in er, one of these er, er, passageways that you servants make such diligent use of. I can see that you are er, er, attending to your, er, duties, with a consummate professionalism, excellent to er, er, see, what, what?" Anna was quite struck dumb by this stammering outburst. He was an odd fellow to be sure.

"Thank'ee sir" she said in reply.

"I have been looking as I er, had er, alluded to er, er, into your family, and a possible connection to several er, er, medieval houses. Franklin Perkins, your husband's father's name was, wasn't it?" his voice suddenly picked up on mentioning her husband's name, until he was almost shouting, despite standing only a couple of paces from her.

"Yes, professor, that is true."

His voice dropped, and he muttered a moment, something that sounded like "finally, finally, the trail of the de Montforts!" before turning back to her, as if he had not paused in their conversation at all.

"Now tell me girl, this is er, er, er, very, very important, I cannot stress that enough, the fates of ancestors and descendants present may depend upon it, what was his father's name, this Franklin, your beloved, er, *husband's father* as it er, were?"

"His father's name was Geoffrey, sir."

"Excellent! And his father before him?"

"His name was Obadiah, sir, a strange name, John told me about it, I never made his acquaintance, him having passed and been buried in the grounds of Harteston Parish Church afore I were brought into this world."

"Splendid! And are there are any others of the Perkins line buried in this er, Harteston Parish, as you say?"

"There are sir, a score or more stretching some way back, and many more before that, I'll wager, though their older graves don't be marked any more. The vicar likes to keep the history where he can, I am sure that he can show you where the graves are, for each of the families buried there."

"I don't believe it! This is remarkable news!" Anna thought maybe she ought to call a doctor. Professor Greenidge did not seem to be in his right mind.

"One final er, er, query if you don't mind, Miss Perkins, did he have a brother, your husband's father? Did your husband have a brother? Or do you know of any other male issue from the loins of goodly, er, Mr. Franklin Perkins, your er, husband's father? Did you have your husband's child perchance?"

"No sir, neither my husband nor his father had brothers. His father had a sister, but no brother. My John, he was the only child of his father and mother I'm afraid. Though, yes I do have a son of my own, born to my late husband."

"A son! Oh, you have a son! Oh this is remarkable, remarkable news, thank you kindly, Miss Perkins! Our paths will no doubt cross again!"

Professor Greenidge shook her hand forcefully, and fairly ran back into the library, leaving Anna feeling more than a little confused.

The next day Anna could not stop herself from thinking about the professor's words. She had initially ignored and dismissed it as a lot of strange, academic babble, but having slept on it, and pondered further what he was trying to express, she could not get away from her internal questions.

What did he mean?

Why on earth could he be so interested in her humble family of farmers down in Harteston?

Why did he keep mentioning them in the same breath as this great medieval family, the de Montforts?

It was certainly an enigma, and one that seemed unlikely to reach any resolution until Professor Greenidge had cleared up his research and explained himself to her in plain English.

There was no light that she could bring to the topic that was for sure.

All day she served drinks and refreshments to the noble guests in the ballroom and drawing room, listening, as ever, to their conversations.

She was concerned that she might overhear some rumour of Viscount Bellham having a tumble with a serving girl, but was pleased that no such hearsay reached her ears.

The noble ladies and gentlemen didn't seem especially interested in the servants at all, as one might expect, but rather spoke endlessly of their own concerns, of balls and parties and matches between people of their own rank.

"I hear that the daughter of the Earl of Derbyshire is to be wed to a Captain of the Guards, heir to a Marquess", said one lady, sipping her tea conspiratorially.

"Yes, I too had heard such rumours, although I had heard as well of some connection to James Blackwood? Evidently there was some complication there"

"There always is with Blackwood" said the first lady, sourly. She pronounced the name with a fierce contempt, tinged with fascination.

Anna had no idea who they were talking about, but knew at once that he sounded like a cad.

"There is speculation that he means to flee the country. No doubt he has disgraced himself by seducing someone he should not, once again."

"No doubt whatsoever! He simply cannot help himself, it is probably best for all of English society if he finds his way into a long exile."

Moving away from this conversation, which it was not her place to either participate in, or even understand, Anna noted that the Viscount did not seem to be present. Indeed, she had not laid eyes on him all day, or exchanged one of their silent smiles and nods. She found she was missing that, rather intensely.

Still, in a way she was relieved - every time she caught sight of him she was filled with swelling, fluttering notions and sensations, that were entirely inconvenient to her ability to carry out her duties, and had to go away and collect herself in private, back in the pantry or kitchens.

Yet, at the same time, she had been sustained by those lingering moments, and reassured that she had not made a terrible mistake.

She needed that confirmation of her place in the man's affections, even though they had regretfully agreed not to be together. It was difficult, she knew deep down that she still yearned for him, and would most likely continue to do so.

She still had not seen him all day when she headed into the billiard room to polish a little silver. There was a selection of old ornaments in there which Lord Stanningfield largely neglected, but which required polishing all the same, for the sake of making a good impression on the guests, if nothing else.

She did not expect to find anyone in the room at this time of day, though it was often occupied by bored young gentlemen come the evening, who would come in for a round of billiards on Lord Stanningfield's great table, or perhaps a round of cards and some drinks, away from the prying eyes of hopeful unwed ladies, their mothers and chaperones.

It was a room apparently without purpose during the daytime, the cues and balls sitting solemnly, like an army formed up in ranks just for the parade square, so Anna was shocked when she walked in and saw Lady Duckington, her skirts pulled up and her petticoats all atumble, being rather roughly 'served', up against the billiard table, by a bare-bottomed young gentleman.

She could not see his face, and the low grunts the pair were producing were indistinguishable from any others, but she knew at once that it was Richard. Lady Duckington spotted her at once and let out a little shriek.

"Aargh! Get out of here at once girl, begone! Can you not see that this room is in use?" she had quickly restored some modesty by pulling her skirt back down, and had a look of horror spread across her face, which was red and slightly sweaty.

The man fiddled with his breeches and turned around, and she saw in an instant that her suspicions were correct. It was Richard, looking at the floor, clearly embarrassed and ashamed.

"You ought to be ashamed of yourself girl, creeping around unannounced in that manner! I shall inform your employer of your insolence at once!"

"Begging your pardon, My Lady, I shan't disturb you any further..." Anna edged back towards the door, horrified at what she had just witnessed. Nevertheless, she was cut off and compelled to stand her ground by a warm, familiar voice, which immediately eased her panic with its surety.

"Now, now, Lady Duckington" Richard said, looking up at them both for the first time.

"It is not for Miss Perkins to feel shame at this encounter, but us. She was merely attending to her duties - we were, in a sense, entirely neglecting ours. I should think it best if we left now, and never spoke of this again."

Lady Duckington made to formulate a reply, but could think of nothing, and with a harrumphing "tut, tut", she swept from the room, followed by Richard.

As he shut the door behind him, he threw Anna a little nod, and a half-smile. It was a small gesture it was true, but one that, despite his indiscretions and the vast social gulf between them, which they were both all too aware of, set her heart racing at the same rate as it had back in the maze.

She was utterly conflicted in her emotions – she felt at once betrayed and cheapened that he could so lightly forget her and turn to that horrible woman for his pleasure, and yet heartened that he had, once again, seen fit to defend her from attack.

Little did she know that Richard was also conflicted, and felt more ashamed of himself than he had for many years.

The look on Anna's face had struck him like a knife to the heart, and Lady Duckington no longer looked so appealing.

There had been nothing caring in their coupling, and he was left with a sense that she had been using him, as much as he was using her, in a desperate attempt to forget his interlude with Anna.

Chapter Nine

That evening, Anna was quietly picking her way along the main corridor on the top floor, feeling deeply saddened. Her earlier encounter had made her feel a deep sense of shame and regret.

It seemed to reflect rather poorly on the character of Viscount Bellham that a mere three days since their love-making in the maze he could be pursuing an illicit affair with another woman, under the nose of her husband, as well as his host, family and friends.

That he could do so with a woman as obnoxious and haughty as Lady Duckington made it doubly distressing. Perhaps her earlier assessment of the man's character had been wrong, maybe he was just a cad and seducer, using pretty ladies of all classes to pursue his own gratification, and then saying fine words afterwards to ease their heart-break.

She felt very foolish and very alone.

Looking up at the portraits of Lord Stanningfield's ancestors she felt herself calling out to them. Had they faced agonies and anxieties of this sort, these great men of history who had founded the house she depended on for employment? They must have done, she thought, they were only as human as I, or as Viscount Bellham.

When they had posed to have their portraits painted they had done all in their power to project a sense of strength, of confidence and right, but inwardly they too must have doubted everything, feared their own tendency to misjudge or make mistakes, and hankered after attractive ladies who seemed to be beyond their grasp.

It was strange, given her lowly birth and station, and her being a woman, but she found herself relating her feeling and her position to these men, and feeling a little better for it. If only, like them, she always had wealth and titles, and protective outer shells like the 15th century suit of armour displayed on the third floor.

All of those privileges of the upper classes must make life a lot easier to endure, she thought.

Rounding a corner she suddenly found herself face to face, not with another portrait of the Stanningfield family, but with a living, breathing member of it, her friend, the former governess and now wife to the Earl, Lady Catherine.

They had established a friendship some time before her unexpected marriage, and remained on good terms.

"Anna!" Lady Catherine exclaimed, pleasantly surprised. "I have not seen you for days! I trust you are keeping well?"

"Very well, yes Miss" Anna replied, before quickly amending, "That is My Lady, I should say, please accept my apology."

"There is no need for such an apology, Miss Perkins, I am only just getting used to the title myself. It feels rather silly really, this suddenly becoming a Lady. I wonder if I shall ever feel at home in the title."

"I am certain you will, Miss, er, sorry, My Lady, why you undoubtedly have the blood for it, and the education, as you yourself have said."

"All that is true, but if I am to be perfectly frank with you Anna, as I should hope you would be with me, I grow tired of all this aristocratic conversation. It is all so formal, so stuffy! These old Lords and Ladies are obsessed with the most absurd and trifling notions, you'd think they have no idea of the affairs and tribulations of ordinary folk! I've been trying to slip away whenever I can, and I'm sure none of them care a jot. I don't think they'll ever entirely accept me but I don't care much for them either."

"I can imagine Miss" said Anna, feeling herself lapse back into the mode of their earlier friendship.

Catherine was so honest with her, she could not help but realise the absurdity of the situation. She was still the same old Miss Thornberry, even if she had now married into the upper ranks of the gentry, and though she was pleased that her friend had gone up in the world, she was also glad that she had kept her head grounded.

"I have quite enough difficulty conversing with the folk from grand old families myself, being but a humble country girl."

"Then neither of us are alone in that" said Catherine, beaming at her. "I am aware Anna, that you have entered into something of a correspondence with Viscount Bellham."

Anna quickly repressed the look of intense shock that suddenly came over her face. Was there anyone at this party who had not heard some rumour or other about her?

"Do not look so surprised, or ask me how I know, I just know, and that suffices between young women. We know the affairs of the heart intuitively."

"Oh, My Lady", Anna replied, "I am so sorry, I pray I have not brought dishonour to your name and house..."

"Don't be silly, Anna, of course you have not. He is a very charming fellow, and very handsome, and from what I know, I suspect he feels as strongly for you as you do for him."

"But My Lady, how could you possibly know anything of it?"

"As I say Anna, a woman's intuition, never underestimate it." Anna was consumed by affection for her friend, but also assailed by questions. What about Lady Duckington? What about her rank?

"Are you aware at all My Lady, of his relations with Lady Duckington?"

"I have witnessed a little of their affair it is true." Catherine's tone was grave. "She is an attractive woman to any young man, though I personally find her conversation very difficult to endure." They shared a smile at this allusion.

"She is, herself, trapped in a loveless marriage against her will, and eager to grab any means of escape, no matter how irresponsible or un-Christian. I would not interpret their interactions as being of much import, it is likely a passing fancy."

"But Miss, how can I possibly hope for more between myself and the Viscount than a passing encounter? I am only a ploughman's daughter, and he is heir to the Earl of Wiltshire. I am nothing next to him, I feel it most profoundly!" she gasped, choking back tears.

She was expressing her deepest fears and anxieties, and it was good to have this sympathetic ear to unload them into.

"It is not unknown for members of the gentry to fish outside of the conventional pond, where affairs of the heart are concerned" Catherine replied, grinning.

"There are one or two recent precedents one could cite. Who knows what stirs within Bellham? It is merely for you to carry on as you were, and exercise the attraction he clearly has towards you as best you can."

"Oh Miss!" Anna burst out of all formality, and gave Catherine a big hug.

They held each other for a few moments, the two Harteston girls, and both felt better for the open continuity of their friendship.

They parted amicably, and Anna allowed herself a moment of optimism.

Maybe one day, she too would find herself the Lady of a great house, swept up in the arms of a man she loved.

70

Chapter Ten

Anna's mind was far too preoccupied for her to sleep that night. She found her way back to her modest room in the servant's quarters, with its bare-board floor and crumbling, white-washed walls. Curling up in bed with her candle extinguished did no good whatsoever for her efforts at sleep, all she could think about was Richard, her Viscount, and her Lady's words of insight and wisdom from a few hours before. Her brain was pulsing, racing ahead of itself and then doubling back.

What did he really feel? Was an affair between them at all possible? And what on earth, if any, was the significance in all this of Professor Greenidge, and his obsession with her family? Was it possible that it might come to something, that there might be something important about John's family, or was he just an eccentric quack with too much time on his hands?

None of these lines of enquiry seemed to head towards any conclusions. She did not know enough, and she had had no opportunity to talk to Richard about his feelings in all of this, beyond their sad conversation as they left the maze. Indeed, she realised with a heavy heart, she might never actually have the chance to speak to him, ever again.

He, with his household staff in tow, would soon be heading back to Wiltshire, and might not grace Havisham Hall with their presence again, or at least, not for years, by which time he might have found a more suitable bride, or simply forgotten the humble serving girl he'd once rolled about with in a maze when he still had wild oats to sow.

Perhaps Lady Duckington's frail old husband would die, and he would end up with her, absorbing, over time, the sneering, arrogant attitude she seemed to have towards everything. It was all too horrible, a shivering anxiety grew inside her, and became a physical sensation that she could not ignore.

Sleep eluded her, and she was overwhelmed by twin desires; an urge to run about frantically and a strong urge to cry. In the end, she found she was too distracted to manage either.

And then, entirely without either expectation or prior warning there came a knock at her door. A jolt ran through her, a strange blend of excitement and panic and she sat up sharply.

She sat in stunned silence for what felt like the passing of an age, entirely unused to being disturbed late at night, aghast at the potential of who might be there - who on earth could possibly want to see her at this hour.

Assuming it was probably Mrs. Cartwright, come to chastise her, or give her some egregious new duty for the morrow, she tremblingly clutched the bedclothes to her and called out.

"Who is it? Come in?" the door creaked as it always did, swinging on its hinge. It swung slowly, and she braced herself for the Housekeeper's thumping Suffolk accent, lathered in decades of experience and a servant's manner. Instead she was startled, astounded, and incredibly pleased all at once to see Viscount Bellham, dressed more simply than usual, and creeping forward cautiously, offering up a tentative smile.

"I really hope I'm not disturbing you too much" he said, almost whispering, closing the door gently behind him. He seemed less confident than usual, clearly in unfamiliar territory, and aware that she might quite rightly not receive him gladly. "I know that you servants need your rest if you are to fulfil your duties."

"Not at all sir" she said. "Why, I was struggling to sleep, and would be glad of a little company." It was not what she had intended to say, but the ingrained habit of not arguing with the nobility, of accepting their wishes and complying, had taken hold, and she found herself welcoming him.

The part of her that was unbearably hurt by his behaviour with Lady Duckington retreated into the background, and she showed him nothing but her polite servant's face.

"It warms my heart to hear this" he said, sighing as he seemed to relax a little. "- and I share your desire for human contact, my bed grows cold on these chilly nights, despite the approach of summer."

He stepped forward, seeming almost to grow in stature as she met his eyes and did not turn away.

She contemplated him, his upright posture, his lush hair, his robust features and compelling, dark eyes, and she could not help but feel the full force of her attraction, the same force that had led her into the maze only three nights ago.

It felt like an eternity had passed since that evening, and yet, at the same time, she knew that it was so recent as to be fresh and clear at the front of both of their minds.

"I wanted to apologise to you properly for what you had to witness earlier, in the billiard room. It was unseemly, and improper, and I regret it immensely. I'm afraid I have been tempted in the past by the advances of Lady Duckington, I am but a weak-willed mortal man, and capable of exercising less control over my baser instincts than perhaps I would like. I pray that you can forgive me."

She smiled at him. This was the first time he had truly let her see the man, not the aristocrat, and she was impressed by it.

His vulnerability made him more endearing, as, in a very different way, it had when she had spilled the jellies onto his coat when they had first met. It was this willingness to be seen as he really was, and his remarkable honesty of speech and thought, that made him so intriguing - that and his devilish good looks.

"Are you going to stand there looking hesitant all night, sir?" she said, playfully, ignoring his plea for forgiveness for the time being. "- there is nowhere to sit but this bed, humble as it is, but I wouldn't want you to catch cold on my account."

He smiled at her, and nodded, and then moved forward with singular purpose towards her. He sank to sit on the bed beside her, drinking in her tumbled hair, no longer hidden by a servant's cap, her deep brown eyes and fresh skin.

Without conscious intent from either of them, they found themselves drawn together, until he kissed her with a softness of touch, but more depth of feeling than she had ever before known, not with him or any other man. Their lips met lightly, not with the vigorous passion of the other evening in the maze, but with an elemental inevitability, like the creeping approach of spring blossom, or the gentle babbling of a mountain spring.

As his mouth caressed hers she felt a slow but very discernible growth of passion within her, a shivering at his touch and flashes of desire in every part of her. Longing flowed into her and she thrust all thought of status, or impossibilities aside, and chose to simply take pleasure in the moment. After all, she might never see him again, painful as that thought was.

"You shall have to make room" he said against her lips, and she shunted over so that he could lie on the bed with her. He wrapped her firmly in his arms and a safe, warm feeling came over her, mingling easily with the newly aroused desire. Her fingers slowly wrapped themselves about his shirt and she dug in, tactile and dextrous, feeling him, expressing her innermost urges with every lingering touch.

The fabric of his shirt and the rippling of his muscles beneath it all seemed to say something unutterably profound, without the need for a single word to be said. She pulled him closer, and he pulled closer to her, they pressed themselves together and were locked at the lips in silent, sensual communion.

Anna was used to desire being somewhat forced upon her, to the simple and rough love-making of a farmer. This was something new, something that felt, though she knew that she was foolish to think it, deep and serious.

She felt herself expand up and out to new dimensions, felt a new sureness in herself and in this act. Her nipples hardened, their sensitive peaks teased by the coarse fabric of her night rail and every hair on her body seemed to stand up with her tingling awareness of his body and her own. She accepted his kisses, and gave back her own in turn.

He responded to her touch as she desired, touching her in return. First he gently brushed the curls of her rich burgundy hair, where it tumbled against her neck, his touch electrifying as his fingers drifted sensually across her skin, to open the top of her night rail to the air.

She shivered as the cool night air touched her heated nipples, and he lifted her breasts firmly, gently sucked at her nipples and licked the delicate skin surrounding them.

She arched back and let feeling take over, her fingers tangling in his hair and pulling to encourage him, to accept what he offered gladly.

Need was rising in her with every touch of his lips, and she could feel his hardness growing against her hip. Her breathing was ragged now and she cried out as he slid his fingers across that most sensitive bud of flesh, teasing her until her hips pushed against him with her helpless need, and finally, he took pity on her and, lightly at first, then with greater speed and dextrous skill, began to pleasure her with his fingers.

Starting in a slow circling motion, he progressed to a steady rhythm, brushing his fingers across her bud again and again, then sliding them into her, repeatedly, skilfully driving her to a new energy in her movements that forced her to snap her head up and forwards gasping his name. Fingers still thrusting, he arched himself and brought his tongue to work with his fingers, until she spasmed against him, crying out her pleasure as she peaked.

She reached for him, as he slid himself up her body, kissing her breasts, and up her neck, to find her lips again. She welcomed his kiss, tasting herself on his lips, amazed at what he could do to her. For all the sensations that had run through her, she felt larger, more whole, more complete and able to move with confidence and pride towards this man, her Richard, heir to the Earl of Wiltshire or not.

Their eyes met, and she was suddenly drowning in the passion that she saw there, the slow certainty of pleasure, of much more pleasure to come. Moving back from her a moment, he slid out of his breeches, and pulled his shirt off, standing magnificent in his nakedness for a moment before reaching for her again.

He pulled her up, pulled the night rail over her head, and stood back again to admire her, strong and slim and beautiful, rounded in all the right places, bountiful breasts and rich mahogany hair tumbling down to her waist. She sat, drinking him in with her eyes, awaiting him. He came back into the bed and they came together with ease, feeling every tiny part of each other's intimacy, connecting deeply, communicating on a whole new level.

He watched her face, as he lifted her hips and pushed into her, in one long hard thrust, and paused, revelling in the sensation, the feel of her around him, the perfection of their joining. Movement began slowly, with steady, rhythmic thrusts, perfectly synchronised in their movements, their bodies becoming a singular whole. Anna had never felt so completely at one with anyone.

Time seemed not to matter. Space did not constrain them. Any concerns of status or work or the world beyond this bed drifted into the ether.

They pivoted as one body, she now on top of him, gradually taking her fill of his manhood with her hips and thighs, moving fluidly with him as support. She went at her own speed, creeping at first, but then picking up, gyrating more fluently and rapidly with every move she made.

He lay still a moment, watching her move above him, enjoying the sensation, then began to move again, arching his body beneath her to thrust up into her, holding her hips in his strong grip and gasping as his pleasure mounted. He curled himself up, catching her nipple in his mouth and she redoubled her efforts as intense pleasure pulsed through her.

Finally, he almost shrieked in a pleasure she knew that she had drawn out of him, and the sound and feeling of his pleasure tipped her over the edge into her own. After a shared moment of pulsing ecstasy, they reluctantly released each other, separate bodies now, and slid down again to lie in each other's arms.

"Thank you, Anna" he spoke softly, his breathing still fast and uneven.

"For what?"

"For giving me sensations I never thought possible." She smiled, and kissed him strongly. Her lips parted, her tongue sought his, and he returned her passion, with more kisses, and gentle nips of her lower lip.

"Well what can I say" she said, some hot little devil moving through her still "- we country girls know a thing or two." She made him laugh, then gently slapped his firm body teasingly. He seemed to have surrendered himself to her this time. It had been the other way around in the maze.

"This can't go on though, can it sir?" she added, seriously now.

"You must return to your estates, and I to my feather-duster. It's been nice, but I think…" she stammered. She was unused to this level of forthrightness, certainly in her own mouth. It was clear though, that this was impossible. "… I think you'd best leave." He let out an odd sound, almost like a groan of pain, and turned swiftly to face her.

"Anna…" he said "I know that it is true what you say, yet it grieves me so acutely to have to hear it. Oh if only you had some name my idiotic family would find acceptable, then perhaps we could find some way." It was his turn now to stop, unfamiliar with the ideas and notions coursing through him.

A strange mixture of utter joy and deep sadness had come over him. For perhaps the first time in his life he had no idea how to get what he wanted, even though it was the one thing that he wanted more than anything.

"Some way to make this feeling last forever, for the rest of our lives. But, I do not know, you may be right…"

"I am right sir, though I say it myself. My name is not great, it is only Perkins, and I have nothing to offer you by way of a dowry save a little homespun wisdom and a talent for baking cakes. Do not worry…" hearing her practical tone, which conveyed resignation and acceptance of the situation, she suddenly stopped herself.

This was not what she truly felt and she knew it.

She too yearned desperately for a solution to their predicament, for a prolongation of their affair, for a way to make moments like this permanent.

It was only because she knew that it was impossible, that, no matter what Catherine had said, there was no happy ending here, that she was trying so hard to be sensible and grounded. She wanted to cry, but stopped herself, knowing it would do no good. She clung to him, unable to speak, knowing suddenly that she would not see him again, not like this, ever.

"If only…" she said at last, whispering in his ear, gently kissing his neck. "If only" and they fell asleep there, bittersweet in each other's arms.

Chapter Eleven

Tomorrow arrived, and with it, what both Anna and Richard knew had to be the end of their affair. Anna rose early to attend to her duties, whilst her lover was still asleep. She planted a little kiss on his cheek and then left him, unsure whether or not she would see him again. Her heart was heavy but, as ever, she found solace in distracting herself with practical concerns. Since she had heard of John's death, she had many times only got through the day by thinking of Sam, and just doing what was needed to survive. This day was no different. She would survive.

At about half past eleven in the morning, she sat in the drawing room, polishing silver. The house was slowly beginning to empty, as some guests departed for their homes, and there were no guests in the room to be disturbed by her working.

She scrubbed and polished vigorously, taking her work very seriously, grateful for it, for it helped her to forget about Richard, and last night's indescribable pleasures. Looking out of the great windows, she saw horses being hitched to carriages, and footmen in various liveries running around with many trunks and cases of luggage. The house party of Lord and Lady Stanningfield was coming to an end, normal life was returning to Havisham Hall.

Out in the distance, beyond the business of the guests and their staff, the grounds stood still, as serene as they ever would be, tall oak trees unbending in the May breeze which disturbed the roses and brought their beautiful scent to her nostrils. Anna sighed, a heavy but happy sigh. If she could not have the man that she loved, for she did love him, she had come to realise, at least she had known his touch, and could hold the memories dear. It was not such an awful life this, when it really came down to it.

She was busy polishing up a serving spoon when she heard a noise behind her, as the door creaked open and somebody came in. Assuming it would be another servant, she did not bother to stand up or turn around to greet the newcomer, but continued in her duty wordlessly. Nevertheless, she was compelled to look up when a familiar voice stammered:

"Er, Miss Perkins, er, er, was it?" it was Professor Greenidge, looking a little sheepish and peering at her from behind his pince-nez spectacles.

"Yes sir, it was" she spoke a little sharply, surprised and unsure of his purpose. "And what might I be able to do for you, Professor?"

"Well, not a lot, er really" he said, fidgeting uncomfortably "- it was more, er, that there was er, er, something I wished to communicate to you. The results in fact, of some of my, er, er, er, research, as it were, er…"

"Yes sir?" Anna was unsure what to think. She had little formal education, and feared that Professor Greenidge wished to engage her in discussion of some deeply academic topic, of which she had no knowledge. Reading came easier to her than to the typical country housemaid, but that was about all that could be said of her education. She had not had the chance to indulge in intellectual pursuits, and feared greatly that she would not understand anything that he might wish to tell her.

"Well, it's like this you see" Greenidge continued "- I'm afraid I may have startled you a little with my er, oddly extensive knowledge of your own family, and er, er, considerable interest in your er, husband's lineage. I must profusely apologise for any er, unnecessary, er, er, consternation this may have caused you, but I er, er, feel that the result of my enquiries will be most to your er, er, pleasant surprise, and er, satisfaction?"

"Whatever can you mean Professor?"

"The de Montforts. That is to say, you are, of the de Montforts, you are er, er, a de Montfort, by marriage, one of the few remaining, er, your husband, was er the rightful inheritor of the de Montfort title, of er, er, Duke of Dorchester, and your little son Samuel is er, er, now the bearer of that title, your husband being sadly, er, deceased, which makes you the Duchess and, er, er, once Samuel marries, that will become Dowager Duchess, of course."

Anna was more than startled. She was momentarily beyond speaking, and sat, frozen in place, as she considered what she had heard. She had really heard that, had she not? It was not just her wishful thinking? Was this really true? Was this a joke? How on earth could it be possible?

"But sir…" she said, getting to her feet, shaking, her mouth wide open in shock. "Professor, how can this even be possible?"

"I presumed you might ask that!" Greenidge was newly animated, as he always seemed to be when discussing his favourite subject. He produced, from the bundle clutched under his arm, a huge document, covered in an intricate web of names, dates and marital connections. "Which is why I took the liberty of drawing this er, er, fairly straightforward and considerably simplified er, chart of the lineage, to demonstrate, the path of descent of the title."

"Simplified?" Anna wanted to say, but thought better of it. She'd not like to see the complicated version, the chart was impenetrable!

"But er, put simply this is your husband's family tree, tracing his lineage all the way back to Simon de Montfort, the renowned, er, Lord and Knight, of the Middle Ages. His line has become somewhat er, confused over the years, you will note the complex web of marital arrangement in the mid-15th century in particular, but your son, or that is to say, your husband's father, er, Franklin Perkins, and therefore your son, now, is the rightful heir to the title, via this chap." He pointed firmly at a name on the chart, a man called Cecil de Montfort-Perkin, in the late 1600s.

"That was a good, er, one hundred and sixty years or so ago, and the rightful heir has not been known until now. I am most pleased, most pleased, to be the one to have finally found a true heir!" Professor Greenidge beamed at her, obviously more pleased for himself than for her.

"I regret to say, there is only a small fortune to come with the title. Little of the family's money has been traced, and much has been used up on er, er, legal fees and such like. What remains is stored in a London safe deposit. Then there are the estates of course – the entailed properties remain, but need upkeep. Anything not entailed was sold or otherwise passed out of the control of the family's men of business long ago."

"How much sir? What do you mean when you say a small fortune?" Anna asked feverishly, assailed by another wave of shock.

"Oh, very little as I say, around three and half thousand guineas, give or take a few, er, er, shillings here and there, with the bankers. And I believe that the estates still produce an income of five thousand pounds a year, but most all of that goes on just barely maintaining the entailed properties. I'm sorry that it isn't more, er, but I suppose it would be enough to restore at least one estate to a modest condition and a pay a few er, critical staff, what?"

Anna was amazed, stunned. Three and a half thousand guineas! And then an income of five thousand pounds a year! She had no idea what great houses cost to run, but surely that was enough. That was more money than she could ever have dreamed of, more than the whole village combined could ever have earned in a lifetime!

And now it was theirs, well, Sam's, along with the title and name of an ancient and noble family. She was noble by marriage – it seemed overwhelmingly improbable…. Yet…. This was incredible.

In that moment she realised that there was one thing that she had to do, right now. She had to tell Richard!

"Come with me Professor!" said Anna purposefully, fairly grabbing Greenidge by the hand and hauling him out of the drawing room. "There's someone who needs to know all this and quickly!"

They ran, Anna as quickly as her legs could carry her, Professor Greenidge stumbling and stuttering behind, his precious family tree diagram billowing in his grasp, holding on to his pince-nez in a most ridiculous manner. They tore down corridors and into the various rooms, surprising and disturbing those guests who were still taking tea and cakes and discussing aristocratic concerns. It seemed that Richard was nowhere to be found. Anna's panic rose the further they went without finding him.

"Begging your pardon!" Anna said, after bursting in on a few old ladies gossiping in an anteroom.

"I should think so too!" one of them said sourly as the exasperated girl rushed out.

"Awfully sorry!" Greenidge saw fit to add, on his way out, as if it excused any kind of mad behaviour. "She's a de Montfort don't you know!"

They hurtled through the main hallway, weaving a path through footmen who were carrying cases and valises outside, barely avoiding old Featherstone the Steward on the stairs (at which point Greenidge, by way of apology, could only manage a short cry of "de Montfort!" which confused all and sundry) up to the guest suites. Anna sprinted to Richard's bedchamber, but only his valet was present.

"Where's Richard, er, that is to say, where might I find Viscount Bellham, good sir?" she panted desperately.

"My master is already at his carriage. I am just bringing down the last of his things. He is to leave Havisham on the hour." Anna looked up at the nearest clock. There were less than five minutes to go until twelve o'clock! She had to find him, as quickly as she could, so she turned around, barged past Greenidge shouting "come on!" into the professor's bemused face, risked her neck dashing down the stairs four at a time and hurtled out of the front door, knocking a large leather valise over as she did so.

There were four carriages assembled outside, but she immediately knew which one was her intended target, for there, giving instructions to a footman and looking splendid in the same light blue coat she had selected for him only five days ago, stood Richard Maitland, Viscount Bellham, the man who she now knew, with certainty, that she loved.

"Viscount Bellham! Viscount Bellham!" she dashed over in a manner unbefitting a lady of her recently discovered rank, but she did not care. She had but one purpose, and she was going to see it out.

"Anna!" Richard said, his eyes gleaming the moment he turned to face her. "It is good to see you, but what is it? Is there something wrong?"

"Professor Greenidge…" she panted, trying as hard as her lungs could manage to take in air and catch her breath "… has discovered… I am… title… what is it er, professor?"

"Well…" said Greenidge, equally exasperated and holding up his family tree "- simplifying tremendously of course, and taking into account several years of dedicated er, er, research, I can confirm that Miss Perkins here is in fact, the widow of er, John, son of, er, er, Franklin, er de Montfort-Perkin, rightful heir to the title Duke of Dorchester via er, er, his descent from the de Montfort family line, making Miss Perkins the Duchess of Dorchester and her young son Samuel, Duke of Dorchester. Delightful discovery, don't you think?"

The Professor beamed at the Viscount, thrilled to have such an attentive audience.

Richard was as shocked as Anna. He looked almost pale with awe at the notion, his eyes and mouth wide open. He stared at her, his mind racing, here he was, having spent the morning desperately trying to find a way that he could marry Anna, even penniless as she was, without being completely disinherited, his heart breaking at their predicament, and now this. It was a miracle, an absolute miracle!

He looked from the professor to Anna, and as they shared a moment of eye contact, the whole situation was just too much and they both broke out into uncontrollable fits of laughter.

"You're a Duchess!" he exclaimed, jubilantly. "You're a bloody Duchess, I don't believe it!"

The professor had begun to sputter his explanations again at these words, but Richard hastily put his mind at rest

"Well, actually, I do believe it, and it's wonderful! There's only one thing for it…" and then suddenly, solemnly, romantically, he dropped to one knee.

"Anna De Montfort-Perkins, will you be my bride?"

"Yes sir! Yes of course I will!" she all but shouted. Richard rose to his feet, pulled her into his arms and embraced her with feelings of utter joy, and kissed her in a way she wanted to last forever more.

About the Author

Arietta Richmond has been a compulsive reader and writer all her life. Whilst her reading has covered an enormous range of topics, history has always fascinated her, and historical novels been amongst her favourite reading.

She has written a wide range of work, from business articles and other non-fiction works (published under a pen name) but fiction has always been a major part of her life. Now, her Regency Historical Romance books are finally being released. The Derbyshire Set is comprised of 10 shorter novels (6 released so far). The 'His Majesty's Hounds' series is comprised of 10 novels, with the fourth having just been released.

She also has a standalone longer novel shortly to be released, and two other series of novels in development.

She lives in Australia, and when not reading or writing, likes to travel, and to see in person the places where history happened.

Be the first to know about it when Arietta's next book is released!

Sign up to Arietta's newsletter at

http://www.ariettarichmond.com

When you do, you will receive a free copy of the <u>subscriber exclusive</u> novella **'A Gift of Love',** a prequel to the Derbyshire Set series, which ends on the day that 'The Earl's Unexpected Bride' begins

This story is not for sale anywhere – it is absolutely exclusive to newsletter subscribers!

Other Books in 'The Derbyshire Set'

Available at all good book stores and for ebook readers too!

Coming Soon!

Books in the His Majesty's Hounds series

Enchanting the Duke (coming soon)

Redeeming the Marquess (coming soon)

Healing Lord Barton (coming soon)

Winning the Merchant Earl (coming soon)

Loving the Bitter Baron (coming soon)

Rescuing the Countess (coming soon)

Attracting the Spymaster (coming Soon)

Here is your preview of the next book in
'The Derbyshire Set' by Arietta Richmond

The Derbyshire Set – Book 4

Regency Historical Romance

The Count's Impetuous Seduction

Arietta Richmond

Charlotte cast her eyes around the church, looking for Don Diego. With a dismayed sigh she realised that he did not appear to be among the guests, here for her sister's wedding. She stifled her sigh so as not to alert the other guests to her desperation. For weeks this had been the only date on her mind, the only day that she could focus on, whenever she looked at a calendar or glanced ahead in her diary. It was today, the twelfth of June 1817, the day that she would be reunited with her Don, yet it had come and he did not seem to be here.

It was almost too much. This might be the greatest day of her sister's life, but she was not sure she could bear it. Risking ruination, she thought about getting up and running out, finding a quiet spot in the shadow of a yew tree, or beside a grave, in which to cry her eyes out.

Despite all of the affection that she had towards her older sister, who was marrying her handsome captain, the joy of the occasion dissipated. It seemed as if all she could imagine of life from here on was struggle and pain.

She had poured over Diego's short note obsessively, ever since it was delivered to her, shortly after he had left for London.. Every word had been scrutinized, every syllable picked apart, ever stroke of his pen analysed for signs of his true feelings. He had addressed her as 'My Lady' but then signed off as 'ever yours', a strange clash of formality that could probably be attributed to him being a foreigner.

Likewise, he had said that he was 'eagerly awaiting the chance to see you again', but in her infatuated haze she could not allow herself to believe that this was an entirely sincere expression. Did he mean it, or was he merely being polite?

Was he really eager about her, or merely about another occasion in the social calendar? It was impossible, trying to start a love affair with a letter, yet in her head it was almost as if she had done everything in her power to do so. She closed her eyes to go to sleep every night and he was there, holding out his hand to her, smiling at her on the dance floor, his flamboyant Latin attire glistening in the candlelight. But he was not here, and that seemed to be all that mattered for the present.

Charlotte, trying very hard to look demure and entirely focused on the wedding proceedings, still desperately craned her neck, trying to get a look around the columns of the church.

It was possible, if unlikely, that she had not seem him entering, and that he was in one of the many nooks and crannies around Tideswell Parish Church that was not visible from where she was sitting, in pride of place beside her mother and father, in the first rank of pews. As her eyes darted around the room they met the gaze of many strangers, and many more relations and friends of the family. There was Lady Staveley, looking fatter by the year, and Miss Henrietta Elmton, still without a husband even after her thirtieth year.

They all looked back at her curiously, presumably wondering why on earth Blanchette's sister was behaving in such a distracted and unseemly fashion on the day of her sister's wedding. All the faces seemed familiar to her, until suddenly, her eye settled on one face, handsome, distinct, masculine, that she had never seen before but immediately wanted to go on seeing, for as long as she dared.

He was seated near the back of the modestly sized church, and seemed to be alone, or as good as. The moment she spotted him she was surprised that she had not noticed him earlier, owing to the fact that he seemed almost to dominate his entire pew, so bright was his shock of red-brown hair. He seemed, from his bearing, his ferociously intense gaze and the half smile that curled the corner of his lip, to be in command of all his surrounds, with that easy swagger that comes to many sons of the nobility. He wore a dark green coat and a richly embroidered waistcoat, topped by a crisp white cravat, all finely tailored, all enhancing his appearance of nobility and confidence.

Charlotte was seated some distance from him, but she could see that he had the most incredible green eyes, of a brighter green than she had ever before seen, looking intently forward, towards the ceremony going on at the front of the church. She could not quite understand it, but she was for a few moments at least, distracted from thoughts of Don Diego, and focussed instead on this mysterious, dashing young man whom she had never seen before. Ignoring all laws of etiquette and sisterly decency, she turned to her mother.

'Mother' she whispered, as loudly as she dared '-who is that fellow near the back of the church with the reddish brown hair? I don't believe I have ever laid eyes on him…'

'Shush girl!' her mother hissed back '- have you no notion of decency? This is your sister's wedding!' and Charlotte noticed Captain Westbury, looking remarkably handsome in his full parade uniform of the guards, twitch slightly at the sound of muttering behind him. The threat of the soldier's fury, and the prospect of her shame-faced apologies to Blanche at the reception party, was enough to silence her. Her mother however, to her immense surprise, had turned around to follow up her interest, despite her earlier recrimination. She saw her look carefully behind, scouring the banks of seats for a sight of the man her daughter had just mentioned.

'I see who you mean' Lady Derbyshire said, directly into Charlotte's ear, with practised discretion. 'I believe that is the Marquess Hemsbridge, from down in Somerset. You'll have to ask your father if you want more detail; he invited the fellow'. Charlotte's interest was piqued.

A Marquess? And yet he looked so young and full of life and energy, to have already come into possession of a great estate and title was most impressive to the impressionable young girl of twenty. Charlotte leaned in towards her mother, and almost as privately, whispered:

'He's rather handsome isn't he?'

'Coarse girl!' came the immediate response, Lady Derbyshire's shock barely contained by her whisper. '- to speak of such things on an occasion like this!' Then however, her mother glanced around for another quick peak at Hemsbridge.

'Between you and me however...' Charlotte barely repressed a giggle at her mother's tone, which would have been especially embarrassing had it escaped. At the front of the church, the Bishop of Derby was just working his way towards the vows. '... I should have to say I echo your sentiment. Don't you dare disclose that to your father however!' They shared a second's grin, and returned to facing the front.

'If any person present...' the Bishop droned on in his reedy, pious voice '... knows of any reason why these two may not be joined together in Holy Matrimony, may he speak now, or else, forever hold his peace.' An awestruck silence descended on the room. Many here had been present at Blanche's abortive wedding a few short months ago, and instinctively, they feared a repeat performance. This time, however, (perhaps owing in part to the absence of one Mr. James Blackwood) nobody spoke up, Captain Westbury held his ground, and Blanche was able to quickly turn the fearful expression with which she had regarded the room into one of happiness and security.

'Lady Blanchette Cavendish, do you take this man, Captain Henry Westbury…' the bishop carried on, and for the first time that day, with her sister finally tying the knot, Don Diego somewhere in England, hopefully pining after her, and that handsome stranger Hemsbridge seated at the back of the church, Charlotte Cavendish felt nothing but happiness at being alive.

Outside, the congregation greeted the happy couple with cheers, a few tears, and showers of confetti. Bells pealed, and despite their friendly rivalry for the attentions of desirable men like Henry Westbury, which had persisted throughout their adolescence, Charlotte was swept along in all the good feeling, and felt overjoyed for her sister. Captain Westbury turned to face the crowd for a moment, with Blanche in his arms, and cried out in his commanding, military voice:

'My Lords, Ladies and Gentlemen! To Amfield!' the guests cheered once again at this, and all at once set about the rather arduous process of each collecting their maids and footmen and making for their carriages. There was to be a great ball this evening, in celebration of the wedding, at a cost which Lord Derbyshire had winced at on principle and then happily paid.

The servants at Amfield had been in a frenzy of preparation to ensure that only the best was provided. Tomorrow, after the celebration was complete, Blanche and her Henry would set off for Italy, for a leisurely and protracted honeymoon which would presumably involve the delicate business of producing an heir...

In the press of bodies that had assembled along the small churchyard path, Charlotte found herself suddenly and unexpectedly separated from her parents, with whom she would be riding back to her house. Momentarily panicked, she tried to raise her small frame upwards to spot them amongst the crowds, but could not.

She was considering calling out when suddenly, as she turned, looking for them, she found herself face to face with Lord Hemsbridge, the man whose eye she had met inside the church, looking even more impressive seen close up, as he strode assertively towards his carriage.

'I beg your pardon, my Lord!' Charlotte could not help but cry out at once. Fixed by his powerful, green gaze, she was suddenly frozen in place, her awareness of the crowd around her fading away, and felt an unfortunate blush creeping up the back of her neck.

He was undoubtedly handsome; she only hoped that he would not notice her sudden redness, or if he did, that he would be enough of a gentleman to pretend he had not, and therefore not embarrass her completely.

'Please, the fault was entirely mine' he said in a crisp voice that did not sound used to waiting around or indulging in idle chit chat.

He gazed at her for a moment, as if he were looking for something in her face, in the depths of her pale blue eyes or the slight kink in her fair hair.

His eyes narrowed contemplatively, and they shared a silent moment of communication, seeming to say all that needed to be said of the attraction that instantly existed between them with their eyes and faces.

'Forgive me' he said, injecting a little more warmth into his tone of voice '- I don't believe we've been introduced' he placed his hand on his broad, toned breast, and offered a slight bow. 'I am Lord Hemsbridge; I have journeyed up from Somerset at the behest of the Earl of Derbyshire. My attendance had been a mere formality but now that I see that with such fair company...' he maintained his piercing gaze, even as he stopped to kiss Charlotte's hand.

She felt a little flutter, somewhere deep inside her. Once again Don Diego seemed for a moment to be but a passing fancy. '- I can see that the trip was not in vain. What is your name, my Lady?'

'I am Lady Charlotte Cavendish' Charlotte replied, trying to be coy and reserved, as Blanche would be when confronted by a handsome gentleman. 'I am the younger daughter of the aforementioned Earl, and also have the privilege of being sister to the bride.'

'You are Lady Blanchette's sister?' Hemsbridge said, promptly. '- and there was I convinced that the fairest of the famous Cavendish sisters had already been wed. It is a bounteous pleasure to make your acquaintance.'

'The pleasure is undoubtedly mutual, sir' said Charlotte, with a pleasantly flirtatious nod that concealed the complex and powerful feelings bubbling up inside of her.

She still felt for her Don, yearned for him even, and yet this man had stirred something in her as well, something irrepressible, and impossible to ignore.

Was love always this difficult, she felt like exclaiming? '- I trust you shall be joining us at Amfield House for the subsequent celebrations?'

'Undoubtedly' he replied, not wasting a single breath. 'I had wondered whether such an attendance would be worth my while, but I can see now...' he regarded her conspiratorially.

She knew that dark look some gentlemen liked to throw out. Charlotte was used to watching other girls receive it, bat their eyelashes and glance away from it tenderly, and it was quite a thrill to finally be on the receiving end. What great mysteries those green eyes concealed!

'... that it would be quite a pleasure.'

'Indeed, my Lord. I must now re-join my carriage; however, I trust you shall have a safe and comfortable passage through the Peaks.'

'As do I' he replied. 'Safe and comfortable indeed.'

They looked at each other, the one contemplating the other, imagining all manner of carnal possibilities in the silent and private parts of their minds.

And then without another word, Charlotte turned, and hurried to re-join her family for the ride back to Amfield House.

Read the rest......

Get

"The Count's Impetuous Seduction"

as soon as it's released – go to
http://www.ariettarichmond.com

and make sure that you are signed up for news and release notices !

Other Books from Dreamstone Publishing

Dreamstone publishes books in a wide variety of categories – here are some of our other bestselling books:-

We have books in many categories, ranging from Erotica and Romance to Kids Books, Business Books, Photography, Cook Books, Diaries, Coloring books and much more. New books are released each month.

Be the first to know when our next books are coming out

Be first to get all the news – sign up for our newsletter at

http://www.dreamstonepublishing.com

9 781925 499544